UNDEAD EVER AFTER

THE ACCIDENTAL REAPER URBAN FANTASY SERIES, BOOK 7

MISTY EVANS

Beach
Path
Publishing

1

*A*t two minutes past midnight, a bullet tore through my heart.

In Shepherd's Rest cemetery, I was surrounded by death, but I hadn't expected to meet my own.

Maybe I should have. It was April Fools' Day, after all. Guess the joke was on me.

I hit the ground hard, knocking my head against a grave marker. Somewhere in the darkness, Andy and Aurora screamed my name. *"Chloe!"*

I also heard it shouted down the telepathic channel I shared with my soul mate, Killion. He felt my shock and pain. His voice echoed in my head: *What has happened?*

Sheer agony tore through my bones, blood, and organs, locking me in paralysis. Clouds threatened rain as Andy dropped beside me, pressing a meaty hand to my chest. His face swam into view. My heart stuttered—once, twice, three times—each beat loud in my ears as the bullet and the fall battled inside me.

Aurora's boots pounded the path. She skidded to a stop beside us and dove into her bag. "Hang on, Chloe."

She yanked out a vial of amber liquid and poured it over the wound. A new burst of sheer torment raged through my chest.

Killion's voice was as insistent as the pain. *Talk to me. Tell me what has befallen you. Do you require help?*

He was thousands of miles away in another country, unable to help me now. I coughed up blood. Black dots swarmed my vision, but all I saw was his face. I loved that face and might not see it again if I closed my eyes, the afterlife tugging on my spirit.

Can I resurrect myself from this? The thought tumbled through my mind, along with plenty of others. I've had brushes with death and been able to revive myself, thanks to my innate necromancy, but whatever was in the bullet lodged in my heart was made for supernaturals.

Shot, I sent back to Killion. There was no point in keeping the truth from him—he could no doubt feel the pressure in my chest even across the distance. *Andy and Aurora are...*

The air around me warped, cutting off my train of thought. Killion and I had gotten married in December and hadn't even celebrated a honeymoon yet. Me: 25. Him: over 300. Marriage goals, right?

Until tonight.

Working for Death and Soul Management Group as a grim reaper had its perks. It also had a downside. An abundance of downsides, actually. Plenty of supernaturals had me on their hit lists.

My job? Reap supernaturals who'd dodged death or

broken Soul Management Group's rules. SMG was going to be pissed that I'd screwed up royally and was about to die. Maybe this time for good.

Along with being the original grim with the power to resurrect myself and others, I was also a strange hybrid, having gone through a vampire turning. My sire wasn't just any vampire—Killion hailed from the line of originals who came from another world and possessed dragon magic. None of us knew exactly how this addition to my powers might emerge from me, but at the moment, neither that nor my grim magic was expelling the bullet.

Andy shook my shoulder. His voice cracked. "Chloe. Talk to us."

My lungs seized. I tried to speak, but only a hiss of breath escaped. Aurora's voice rose sharp and fast as she barked into her phone—probably calling Katarina and Harlow, the rest of our hunting party. They were assisting us in searching for a rogue shifter/vamp who'd been killing humans. Andy scooped me into his arms and ran, wolf-fast, toward the limo. But I knew it was too late. My only hope was that necromancy would bring me back.

I love you, I told Killion. *In this life and the next.*

My body shut down. One system after another blinked out, and cold swept through me—the unmistakable hand of death.

If I didn't resurrect myself, Killion would die, too, but the bond between us would never break. Even when the afterlife claimed one of us, the other was destined to follow.

It was my last thought before I died.

. . .

Raising yourself from the dead isn't fun. It's disorienting, painful, and my brain continues to glitch off and on for hours later.

When I came to around sunrise, the bullet had been removed, and my chest was bound with thick bandages. I floated in a haze for a bit, a dreamscape of fuzzy, odd images. Their emotions hit like hail—anger, fear, endless questions. My brain wasn't online, and dealing with them felt as if I was running through a haunted house—all I could do was keep going.

At least I was in the giant bed I shared with Killion at his penthouse suite in the Beaumont Hotel in Danté's Grove, Louisiana. As per usual when I first regained life, I sucked in a giant breath, then winced at the agony that tore through my ribs.

After freezing and blinking away the fog, I groaned and sat up. Memories flooded back, and my body vibrated with clashing magics.

I glanced around, pushing hair from my eyes and searching for my husband. Instead, I found my boss twiddling his thumbs beside the bed.

"About time," Death said, rising to his feet from the chair he'd pulled up next to me. No accent this morning, but his usual scowl was firmly in place. "That one took longer than usual."

I rubbed my bandaged chest. "Sorry to keep you waiting. I know how inconvenient my deaths are for you."

He ignored my sarcasm. "Fang Boy will be back soon. He's wrapping up our latest catch."

I rubbed my ribs gently. "Is he okay?"

"Outside of putting a bulls-eye on Kildare because he

4

was scared you were *dead* dead, he's his normal broody, cranky self."

A relieved sigh escaped my lips. "Why didn't you... you know, bring him with you?"

"You know that's against the rules."

Rules. SMG was drowning in them. "They could've made an exception. Just this once."

"Not without Mei's sign-off. She said no."

So he *had* asked. That pleased me. "Of course not. She hates me."

"You're not her favorite person," he agreed. "Since Romania, neither is Fang Boy."

Killion hadn't meant to turn me. The Board knew that. So did Mei. "She owes me for bringing you back from the dead."

He winced, not appreciating the reminder of what had happened to him in Romania. "That's not how she sees it."

Semantics. "Kildare snuck up on me." Several shades had been hanging around—souls who'd died before their soul contract was up—and trying to possess humans during the weekend ghost tours. It would have been a routine clearing with Andy and Aurora until Kildare appeared, and I called in backup to help us take down the shifter-vamp.

"You got sloppy."

My vampire-dragon blood burned like lava. Ash coated my mouth. I could almost taste fire. Well, if my chest and ribs hadn't been killing me, I might have. My supernatural abilities would speed the healing soon enough, and I'd be hunting down Kildare.

If Killion didn't get to him first.

"What did he shoot me with?" I croaked. "That was no ordinary bullet, was it?"

"Something we haven't seen before," Death said. "The nerds at Smudgy are analyzing it."

Smudgy was his nickname for SMG. Ghost bounded in, ears flopping, and leapt onto the bed with a flurry of kisses. The five-pound white Papillon mix, with ears as large as satellites, placed her paws on my shoulders and slobbered enthusiastically all over my face. Flinching at the pain it caused, I petted her and glanced at the clock. "Oh, man. I barely have time to eat before I have to get to the clinic."

My six-foot-seven boss put his hands on his hips and glared down at me. "You just died. Again. You're in pain. Kildare is still out there. He could try again."

I shifted Ghost onto the sheets and peeled back the covers. It took everything I had not to yelp when I swung my legs around. Just that much movement caused my chest to flare with agony again, shooting the pain into my back and down my spine. It took a second for me to regain my breath. "He's not going to walk into the clinic and shoot me in broad daylight. I'll handle him after nightfall. That's when he'll be out again."

"You're falling behind on your grim cases. The clinic is taking too much of your time."

I braced myself on the edge of the mattress before I gathered enough strength to stand. Another wave of pain rattled through me, but I also felt my magic waking up to counteract it. I needed to eat and refuel both my physical and supernatural bodies. "We're too busy. I'm doing the best I can and will take care of all my cases. Are you staying for breakfast?"

He knew I didn't want him to, and I could see him debating whether to ruin my day or not. "I have reports to file." He scanned me from head to toe. "Try not to die again today, okay?"

I gave him a thumbs up and sighed with relief when he vanished.

 *L*ife is complicated enough when you're a grim
reaper. Marry a vampire master, and your life
gets ten times more so.

An hour after I arrived at the clinic, Raleigh Torlino
and his horned dragon, Sir Isaac Newton, glared at me
from the other side of the reception desk. "I'm part of the
nest," Torlino snarled softly. "I'm exempt from the *waiting*
area."

I handed him a clipboard with our standard intake
form. "No one is exempt. All these people have appointments. Next time, you should make one, too."

The dragon offered a neutral, unblinking expression.
It wasn't often I got to work on such creatures, and I was
excited at the prospect. Still, his vampire owner needed to
understand that his connection to my husband did not
give him preferential treatment.

Torlino hissed. "Your disrespectful and discourteous
treatment will be reported."

He took the dragon and left. I knew he wouldn't get

far with Killion, but it might be fun to see him try. I sent a mental message to my husband. *When Raleigh Torlino requests a meeting with you, I want to be there.*

His response was immediate. *Your wish is my command.*

I liked it that he didn't query me about what had transpired. He knew I didn't create issues with his nest unless they deserved it. We'd already had a long telepathic conversation during my quick breakfast and drive to the clinic. I'd assured him I was fine; he assured me he knew I was still in pain. He'd also told me that Katarina, Harlow, and several of his trackers were hunting down Kildare. They were aware of the new bullets and were taking precautions.

A ferret was running amok among the waiting crowd. "Mr. Montgomery, please keep Whiskers in his carrier," I called. "The last thing we need is a game of hide and seek under the cabinets." I juggled three patient charts. My other hand typed prescription info into the computer. My body was healing, but I was still sore. Every once in a while, a wrong twist shot pain through my ribs. If multitasking while pretending to be fine were an Olympic sport, I'd take home the gold.

The office phone rang for what felt like the millionth time. I lunged for the receiver, tucking it between my ear and shoulder as I continued typing. "Frosty Paws Veterinary Clinic, this is Chloe speaking. How may I help you?" On the other end, a hysterical woman rattled off a string of sentences that all ran together. From what I could decipher, she was convinced her cat had swallowed a rubber duck. An *entire* rubber duck.

I bit my lip to keep from sounding incredulous. "Mrs. Lowe, I'm sure Dudley couldn't—" I paused, reconsidering, as I set the charts down. I'd seen many unusual things during my tenure as a veterinarian, and having been the daughter of two veterinarians before that, it'd given me extensive experience with such situations. A determined pet could accomplish the unthinkable. And this was the same cat that once ate an entire tube of glitter glue. "You know what? Bring him in. We'll squeeze you in around..." I checked the appointments. There wasn't even breathing room, much less an open time for another exam. I'd have to make it work. "Is noon okay?"

Mondays at the clinic bring their own kind of chaos. April Fools' Day seemed to multiply the pandemonium. I never knew why, but it was like a super full moon—people and animals got a touch wild. Add in the fact that the weather had gone from a reasonable fifty-degree high yesterday to eighty today, and folks were shedding layers of clothes like the dying houseplant on my desk was losing leaves.

My waiting room resembled a zoo. Barking dogs, hissing cats, and a squealing guinea pig kept up the racket while a parrot in the corner squawked loud enough to make my ears hurt. The cacophony nearly made me consider a career change, but then a golden retriever caught my eye as it wagged its tail, and I remembered why I love my job.

The computer dinged with a notification about a patient's blood work. I scanned the reception area for the owner, spotted her, and waved her over to the desk. "Fluffy's blood work came back normal." I shuffled the cat's chart to the top, grabbed the printout, and slipped it inside while the woman thanked me profusely and hugged her long-haired tabby.

My regular office manager, Patty, had eloped with her boyfriend, leaving me to juggle the roles of doctor, technician, and front desk receptionist all in one. My parents, who had opened this clinic twenty years ago and were no longer with me, would have been proud—or horrified—at the current chaos.

As the woman left, I grabbed my iced caramel mocha latte from behind me and took a desperate gulp. I was running on caffeine and too few hours of sleep, but I promised myself I would get through the day. I had a plan for trapping Kildare that night if the vampires didn't hunt him down first.

With some quick maneuvering, I'd handed over one of my backed up reaper cases to my intern, Diego. There was simply no way I had time to handle them all, and he needed more experience. I wanted to send him after Kildare, but that new-fangled bullet had stopped me. This case required extra caution.

My stomach growled, reminding me that my breakfast was already fading. A white chocolate fudge cookie sat in my bag, calling my name. *Soon*, I promised my stomach.

It gurgled back, not believing me.

I called the next patient on the list—the golden retriever, Max, who greeted me warmly before I directed him and his owner to Exam Room Three. Just then, Dr. O'Leary burst out from the surgical area. "Are you going to be able to do the anesthesia?"

He was handling an emergency surgery on a poodle mix that had injured itself chasing a raccoon in the backyard. The X-rays showed a broken leg that required pins. I'd been searching for a regular anesthesiologist for our surgeries, but none of the candidates had answered my help-wanted ads.

We typically schedule surgeries once a week on Thursday mornings. Emergencies, however, are an exception. "As soon as I find someone to cover the front desk, I'll be there. Nita is on her way. She has fifty minutes between classes, and I'll be all yours."

He grunted and returned to the back to wash up. My best friend was nearly finished with her college classes and would be taking her boards in a few months. In the meantime, she worked part-time for me, along with two teenage interns.

Heading back to the front, I noticed a newcomer. A black mastiff and his owner had taken Mrs. Robinson's spot, but before I could ask them to sign in, my other doctor and childhood friend, JR, grabbed me. "Colorado has a tumor. Mammary gland. I need to remove it and spay her."

Another emergency surgery. Great. "Here's what I need," I told him. "You help Dr. O'Leary with his surgery first—a canine with a broken leg needing pins. As soon as you're done with that, he can help you with Colorado."

JR, who was usually easy-going, didn't like putting his surgery second to Dr. O'Leary's. He started to argue, but stopped when the waiting room symphony reached a crescendo. "I'll scrub up after I get Colorado settled in a kennel."

One fire semi put out.

The mastiff and his owner once again caught my attention. The man slouched in a weathered leather duster coat that reached his boots. He looked as though he had walked straight out of an old Western, and the mastiff was one of the largest I'd ever seen, with intelligent eyes that took everything in at once.

Before I could reach them with an intake form, Mrs. Jacobson's teacup Yorkie started yapping at my ankles. "Georgie, you know I love you, but could you please save the Napoleon complex for later?" I scooped up the tiny dog, who licked my chin in excited forgiveness. To his owner, I said, "I'll be with you in a minute." She mumbled apologies as she took the Yorkie back, cradling it on her lap. The phone rang, and I almost tossed the clipboard at the stranger in the duster. I knew he wasn't a regular, and no mastiff was listed on our appointments that morning. "Please fill this out and bring it to the desk when you're finished."

I rushed over to snatch up the receiver, only to realize it was my cell. I shuffled papers until I found it buried under a stack. It was my supplier with an update on our back-ordered vaccines. Important, but it would have to wait. I sent her to voicemail.

"If only I could clone myself," I said to no one in particular.

Ghost appeared at my feet, tilting her head in a questioning glance. She often seemed to read my mind, and her dark eyes showed sympathy. I gave her a quick pat. "Although two of me might just cause twice the trouble."

She barked playfully in what sounded like agreement.

I gave Max his check-up and sent him and his owner on their way. Snagging a bite of cookie, I grabbed the next patient file off my stack. "Whiskers Montgomery? We're ready for you." At least, I hoped we were. JR should have Colorado out of room one by now.

My grim senses tingled as I led Mrs. Montgomery and Whiskers to the exam room. I hesitated for a moment, scanning the woman, but my palm did not itch for my scythe, and my grim tattoo did not heat up. She appeared completely human, and it appeared her soul contract wasn't up.

I breathed a sigh of relief as I shut the door, questioned her about Whiskers' issues, and palpated the ferret's abdomen. Sure enough, it was swollen and tender. Whiskers had eaten the fur off a stuffed animal. If I could use an endoscope quickly, I could probably remove the fabric before it got lodged in his intestines, saving the little guy from surgery.

First, I needed X-rays to determine precisely where the fur was and ensure it had not already entered the lower stomach.

Leaving the front desk unstaffed made me nervous, but I had no choice. I assured Mrs. Montgomery that I would return in a moment to retrieve Whiskers, then made my way back to the desk. Patient privacy was critical, so I stacked files and turned off the computer. I carried the files, phone, and latte to the private office before retrieving the ferret and bringing him to the machine.

He was a ball of energy, and I needed to settle him down because I couldn't hold him and run the machine simultaneously.

Nita came through the back door, calling my name. I responded, and a moment later, she donned an apron and joined me at the X-ray machine. "Do you want to hold him, or do you want me to?"

I could have hugged her. We worked together so well that the X-ray was done in a minute, and I could see on the screen where the fur was trapped. It was high enough in the stomach that the endoscope could access the material with ease, eliminating the need for surgery.

"He needs sedation, and I'll need the endoscope," I told her. She nodded before putting the ferret in a cage so she could prep for the removal.

I ran to the front just as a loud, gurgling croak—not from the parrot—grabbed my attention. Corvus, my midnight-black raven, swooped down the hall, his claws raking across the top of my head and sending my hair flying before he entered the reception area.

I hurried behind him and saw Mrs. Robinson clutching Fluffy to her chest. Corvus did nothing except perch on the reception light fixture, nearly knocking it over as he glared at the bull mastiff.

The man had not filled out the intake form. "Sorry about that," I said to Mrs. Robinson and the rest of the folks who looked terrified by my bird. I stroked his glossy feathers, and he hopped onto my shoulder, his talons gripping me through my scrubs. I tried not to wince behind my smile, attempting to convince everyone that the bird was harmless. He was, mostly. If they'd known he was able to discern death, just like Ghost, and help me cross souls, they probably would have stopped bringing their pets in for check-ups.

Corvus brushed his beak near my ear and clearly communicated, *Dead*.

That's when I felt the tingle again. I glanced around the room, but none of the animals appeared distressed. None of their owners did either. "Who?" I murmured as I pretended to be busy typing on the computer. Many of the patients still watched both me and the bird.

Ghost hopped into my lap. When her eyes met mine, I saw the psychopomp behind them. She was ready to harvest a soul, but the other telltale signs that I needed to do so still had not appeared. My palm felt completely normal, as did my tattoo.

Then, I heard Death's voice in my head. *Two supernaturals have just been in a car accident. They are confused and need to cross over.*

"Kind of busy here," I murmured. "Can't you handle it?"

Death is a demanding boss. *Alley. Now.*

You are messing with my life. I'll send Ghost, but I have to take care of the clinic.

Taking the raven and dog with me, I let both out the back door. They knew what to do.

The next hour passed in a blur. The poodle received its pins, I removed the ripped stuffed animal from the ferret, and Colorado ended up tumor- and ovary-free.

I was exhausted. I finished off my watered-down latte while JR walked one of our clients to the front door, patting her on the shoulder. "I promise Reba is going to be fine," he said in his comforting southern voice. "I grew up with seventeen cats on our farm. I knew more about feline health by age ten than most people learn in a lifetime. Your cat is a fighter." I smiled as I watched him work his magic, and the cat's owner left with her own smile.

By that time, Dr. O'Leary was handling a Burmese mountain dog that had gotten into some chocolate Easter candy. The activated charcoal was already doing its job. Since O'Leary had once been one of my professors, I could almost hear him explaining to the owner, *"Theobromine toxicity looks scarier than it is when caught early. You did the right thing by bringing him in immediately."*

JR took the next patient, and Dr. O'Leary appeared, handing me a file. "By the way, I moved Mrs. Hemsworth's parrot appointment to tomorrow. She said it was no problem, and that thing was making enough racket to wake the dead. Megan said she'd drop by after school to help with the filing."

"You're a lifesaver," I told him.

The door chime rang, and my blood heated. A momentary silence interrupted the cacophony as if all the animals understood who—and what—was coming through the door.

The world around me slowed as I took in the most beautiful sight I'd seen in a week. Killion stood in the doorway, his tall frame silhouetted against the late morning sun.

My heart fluttered and my pulse skipped. Although he was three centuries old, he was unbelievably handsome, dressed in a tailored charcoal suit that looked as if he had stepped out of a luxury magazine rather than off a transatlantic flight. "Killion," I breathed, abandoning the stack of charts.

Ghost yipped excitedly and rushed to greet him while Corvus croaked a hello from his perch in the corner. They had both returned only a few minutes after I had sent them to the alley, and I hadn't heard a word from Death, so I assumed the soul transfer went off without a hitch.

I crossed the waiting room, ignoring the curious stares, and launched myself into Killion's arms. He caught me effortlessly, and his lips met mine. His familiar scent —a blend of warm caramel and old libraries—washed over me, and I instantly felt calmer and less frazzled. My chest didn't hurt at all.

"*Dragă mea*," he murmured against my lips, his faint Romanian accent more pronounced after his time abroad. "I take it you missed me."

"Only slightly less than oxygen," I replied. "You're early. I thought you weren't getting home until tonight."

His knowing eyes scanned the clinic before returning to land on mine. I felt him absorb every bit of me, just as I was soaking in every bit of him. "After what happened, I needed to get home as soon as possible." He and Death had been tracking members of a supernatural gang called The Wild Hunt—wraith-like creatures we had encountered during our wedding in Romania over Christmas. Their leader was the one who'd tried to kill Death—well, technically, he *had*, and I'd restored that life. We'd taken care of Eriling, but his minions had escaped, and Death and Killion, along with Killion's father, had been searching for them across the globe ever since. "I have earned a few days off."

"Excellent," I replied. We couldn't discuss my temporary demise or Kildare with a human audience. "I'm happy to have you home." I silently hoped I could bargain with SMG for a few extra days with him before he had to leave again. I'd make it a make-shift honeymoon.

Mr. Wilson's Maltese barked at Clara Kart's goat, and the phone started ringing again. "It is fortunate I returned sooner than anticipated," Killion said. "Although I must admit, this isn't the homecoming I anticipated. How are you feeling?"

"Good as new," I lied.

"Can you get away early? We have some catching up to do."

I bit my lip as an idea formed—an idea I knew he would hate. "How are your typing skills?" I tugged him toward the desk. "Patty and Frank eloped. The ministroke he had two weeks ago scared her. She isn't taking any chances that he won't be around to see his dreams of going to the Grand Canyon and owning an animal sanctuary. I can't blame her, but I'm struggling with the lack of help."

Killion's expression shifted subtly, as it did when weighing his options. "Call one of the others to take her place until you can hire someone full-time."

"Gee, I wish I'd thought of that," I replied, though I didn't mean to be so dismissive—it had already been a *long* day. I apologized and gave him the rundown on everyone who wasn't available, which was everyone. "I only need you to run things until Megan arrives this afternoon. Diego might even be able to fill in sooner. Please?"

He glanced at the overflowing waiting room, then back at me, resignation settling over his face. When not working on cases for SMG or his own investigation service, he managed an investment portfolio worth billions and had led his vampire family through centuries of conflicts. Now, he was being asked to answer phones and schedule appointments for puppies.

His gaze paused on a bloody scratch down my left arm. "You're injured."

"Haven, the cat, got me. She's quite expressive."

"And you're starving," he observed, tuning in to my current physical state again. "Did you not eat enough breakfast?"

"I did, but I've burned through it."

He could tell everything about me, thanks to our bond *and* the fact that he'd share his blood with me. Yes, I was technically a vampire, but something about my supernatural abilities kept me from becoming a full-fledged blood sucker. *Thank the universe.*

Don't get me wrong. I love Killion, and being his soul-mate is incredible, but personally, blood repulses me. That's one of the reasons I hand off surgeries as often as possible to the other two doctors. "I'm fine," I insisted, ignoring the jitteriness in my left leg that told me I'd had too much caffeine and sugar.

Killion carefully removed his jacket, folding it over his arm before rolling up the sleeves of his crisp silver shirt. The action felt oddly intimate, like watching a warrior prepare for battle. "I'll stay for an hour and locate someone to handle the desk," he said, "but only if you eat something substantial while I'm here."

A familiar, pleasant sensation bloomed low in my belly. I resisted the urge to throw my arms around him again, but I made sure to send a few indecent images across our mental link, expressing my gratitude and promising him a future show of that appreciation when we were alone. "Thank you. Seriously. The appointment system is ancient, and whatever you do, don't let Mrs. Schmidt reschedule again—she's already postponed her terrier's dental cleaning four times. He has an infected molar that has to come out, or he's going to end up really sick."

He settled into Patty's abandoned chair, looking ridiculously out of place—a vampire master surrounded by cartoon dog stickers and pastel appointment cards. He eyed the computer with faint suspicion. "I assume there's a manual for this?"

"It's more...intuitive," I replied.

His expression told me exactly what he thought of that answer, but he simply nodded. "Go. I'll manage it."

I started for the exam rooms, glancing at my vampire husband as he answered the phone with perfect professional courtesy. I caught his eye, and the faint smile he gave me, full of heart, exasperation, and devotion, made me fall in love with him all over again.

3

$\mathcal{K}$illion was still at the desk when lunchtime rolled around. I glanced up from the patient whose ear infection I was checking in the reception room, as all the exam rooms were full, to see a flash of platinum-blond hair on a striking woman who strode into the clinic like a model.

Harlow wore dark jeans and a fitted black blazer that screamed, *I could buy this place if I wanted to.* She scanned the room and me with a look of superiority. I couldn't tell if she was disgusted or intrigued by the challenge we presented. "You called?" she said to Killion.

She was his second-in-command and had managed the clinic while we were on our trip to Romania. While she had the air of an ancient, revered vampire, animals seemed to like her.

Both domesticated and wild animals tend to retreat or become aggressive around supernaturals, which is another reason I have to be cautious about who I hire. Megan O'Leary is the only human who works here and knows the truth about me, Killion, Aurora, and Andy. Since she was dating Mason, a vampire whom Killion thought of as a son, she was cool with it. She hadn't shared this info with her dad, though, and I was relieved.

"Thank heavens," I said, scratching Mrs. DeMarco's coonhound behind his infected ear. To her, I said, "I'll get you a prescription for some drops. Twice a day, every day until they're gone. If he's still having issues after that, bring him back for a recheck. You need to keep his big back foot out of the ear, too, so I'll send you home with a cone collar."

The older woman hugged me before I scribbled on my prescription pad and handed the sheet to her. We had to upgrade to a computerized system soon. All this paperwork was killing too many trees and creating space issues.

My husband stood, not hiding his relief as he relinquished the office chair to Harlow. "You're in good hands now," he told me, snatching up his jacket. "I'll see you at home."

As he disappeared out the door, barely pausing to kiss my cheek, I glanced at my new assistant. "You'd think answering the phone and scheduling appointments was worse than death."

Harlow looked about as excited as Killion had been. "Can't say I blame him."

"It's just until Diego and Megan get here."

"Hmm," she said, sitting and frowning at a dried puddle of spilled latte.

But in less than twenty minutes, she'd reorganized the waiting list, calmed a frantic woman with a rat who'd eaten a paperclip, and somehow convinced Mr. Benson that his appointment would be better moved to the following afternoon. The phone stopped ringing endlessly because she answered the calls so quickly, her voice professional, courteous, and reassuring.

"She's good," JR whispered as we passed in the hallway.

I nodded. "If only I could hire her full-time."

Midafternoon rolled around, and we'd cleared most of the waiting room. I had time to breathe. I ducked into the break room to grab a water and found a fresh, cold caramel mocha latte waiting for me alongside the paper bag with the partially eaten cookie. The latte came from The Smoking Bean coffee shop, where I used to work while attending college. Someone had written GG on the cup.

Short for Grave Girl.

Not many supernaturals called me that, so even if I hadn't recognized Moss' fat printing, I would have known it was from him. He must have slipped into the back room when he picked up Killion to drive him home. Moss was a chauffeur and so much more.

At precisely three, Die burst through the back door like a whirlwind in skinny jeans and a vintage band T-shirt. His long hair was slightly windswept, and his dark eyes were wide with excitement, although devoid of their usual black liner. "You're not going to believe what happened with Darwin Fiskers." He stopped short when he noticed Ghost sitting by my feet. "Oh, hey, girl."

In his world, being a grim reaper was all he had. I

peeked around, ensuring no one was nearby to overhear our reaper talk. "You got him, right?"

Die dropped into the chair across from me, leaning forward, conspiratorially. "Did you know he's been dodging his contract for eighty years? The file said he'd been hiding out in this dive bar in the warehouse district, calling himself 'Moon Dog,' of all things."

I had just taken a sip of latte and snorted it through my nose. "You've got to be kidding." I hastily wiped coffee off my shirt. "And he thought that was cool?"

"I know, right? Anyway, I walk in all casual"—he demonstrated with a gesture that was anything but casual—"and he takes one look at me and bolts. Literally jumps over the bar, knocks over this giant barrel of pickles, and shifts right there."

"In front of the humans?" I whispered, horrified.

"Everyone was so drunk already, they thought it was an April Fools' prank with, like, special effects or something. They clapped and threw dollar bills at him." Die ran a hand through his hair, trying to tame it. "I had to chase him down the street, and he ducked into—you're not going to believe this—that new cat café by the park."

I pressed my palm against my mouth to stifle my laughter, picturing the scene.

"A dozen or so terrified cats, one werewolf, and a bunch of humans screaming at the top of their lungs." His chuckle turned into a full-on laugh. "Let me tell you, it was ugly. Death showed up just as the werewolf knocked over this tower of cat beds and got tangled in the feather toys. Should've seen his face. Death's, I mean. He was furious. You know that eyebrow tick he gets?"

I knew it well. He usually got it when he was around me. "But you *did* reap Fiskers, right?"

"That's the best part." His grin was bigger than the Cheshire cat's. "A huge, orange tabby got so mad at all the commotion that it jumped on Fiskers' head." He mimed claws digging into the werewolf's skull. "He was so distracted that I had no problem touching him with my scythe. Hal took his soul to the afterlife."

Hal was Diego's psychopomp, a hamster with three equal bands across its body, two black and one white. 'Hal' was short for Halloween. If I'd been naming him, it would have been something more obvious, like Oreo.

I fist-bumped him. "Another case closed."

"You should have seen the café owner trying to explain to his customers that the dog and the cosplayer with the fake scythe were part of a promotional stunt." He wiped an imaginary tear from his eye. "Death did that thing where he freezes time for everyone except us, but the cat that attacked the Fiskers stared right at us while Hal did his thing. I swear that feline could see through the veil."

"Some animals can," I said, scratching Ghost in her favorite spot under her throat. "They're more perceptive than humans give them credit for."

Die nodded, suddenly serious. "Being a reaper is wild. I never thought I'd say this after what my sister did to me, but... I think I'm good at this job."

That was a stretch, but the vulnerability in his voice touched me. He'd come a long way from the broken soul I'd first met, forced to possess many different bodies to feed his power-hungry sister. "You're getting better at it," I assured him. "And now I have another job for you."

He stood up and clapped his hands, rubbing them in anticipation. "Whatever you need."

I glanced at the clock on the wall. "Dr. Banks—JR—you remember him?"

"He's the guy who likes horses and is dating your friend."

"That's the one. He's doing a series of vaccines for my former landlady, Vera, and her sister, Velma. They have new rescues they're fostering. I need you to handle the desk and keep all those records straight while answering the phone. Do you think you can do that?"

He gave me a mock salute. "I'm on it."

"Don't tell any of your reaper stories. Today, you need to act completely human."

He held up several fingers. "Scout's honor."

The gesture was not the correct salute, but that was the least of my problems. As he took off for the front desk, I drained the last of the coffee and steeled myself for the remaining hours of this April Fools' Day madness.

The thought of going home to the Killion buoyed my spirits. *I might survive this day after all.*

THE CLINIC WAS BLESSEDLY quiet as I closed the last chart of the day. Ghost stretched beneath the desk while Corvus preened on top of the bookshelf, his beady eyes tracking my movements.

I heard the squeak of the back door. Nita appeared a

moment later in my doorway. "You look like death warmed over, girl. That bad, huh?"

I gave her a wan smile. "It's looking up since you're here, but you missed JR. He already left."

"Can't I visit my best friend?" She plopped down in the visitor chair, her purple hair loose around her shoulders. "He's picking me up for dinner later. I thought I'd better check on you." She glanced at her watch. "You've been here, what, twelve, thirteen hours?"

"I lost count after the great dachshund debacle around four."

"I heard Killion's home. Why aren't you two having a proper reunion instead of you sitting here alone, drowning in vet charts? I can help with those tomorrow."

"Because April Fools' Day decided to live up to its reputation." I sighed, leaning back in my chair and stretching carefully. My ribs were much improved, but I still felt an echo of pain around my heart muscle. "I swear the universe conspired to make *me* the fool today."

She toyed with the edge of her scrub shirt, which had cartoon cats wearing sunglasses. "Well, the conspiracy is over. You need to go home. Like I said, I can tackle those charts tomorrow."

"I have to keep an eye on several of our patients who are here overnight. They're doing fine now, but things could change in an instant. I think I'm going to sleep on the couch."

"You're leaving." Nita left her seat and spun my chair around so I faced her. "Your best friend, who suffered through organic chemistry with you, is telling you to go." She smiled and winked. "I'll have JR bring dinner here. After that, he can help me study for my final tomorrow."

"I don't know..."

"Everything's under control, Morticia." It was her favorite nickname for me. "The world won't end if you take a break. JR and I will keep an eye on the pets. They'll be fine."

Ghost came out from under the desk and barked. "Fine," I conceded, standing and stretching again until my back cracked. I was ready for some Killion and ice cream in bed. "But call me if—"

"If anything catastrophic happens. Like an actual asteroid hitting the clinic. Otherwise, enjoy your night off." She gave me another wink. "You haven't seen your husband in a week. If you don't get out of here, he'll be busting in here to throw you over his shoulder and kidnap you."

I gathered my things. Ghost and Corvus followed me to the back door. When I opened it, Killion stood there with an overflowing bouquet of lilacs, roses, and lilies of the valley, along with a bottle of champagne. "Good," he said. "I see Nita was successful, and I don't have to seduce you into coming home."

From behind me, she waved at him and called, "Mission accomplished."

I grinned. I had my own mission now. It involved a shower, food, and fulfilling my earlier silent promise to show him my depth of appreciation. *I can't wait to get you out of that expensive suit.*

His lips curved into a wolfish grin. *I assure you, it will be my pleasure to submit to your wildest desires.*

"Bye," I said to Nita and raced for the limo.

4

The ride to the penthouse was mostly quiet, due to the fact that Killion and I were locked in a long, passionate kiss.

Ghost had bedded down on the limo's padded leather seat, and Corvus rode up front with Moss.

When I finally stepped out of the elevator into the penthouse a few minutes later, kicking off my shoes with a groan of relief, the place smelled like a seven-course meal. Pennyworth, Killion's butler and cook, had exactly that waiting for us.

I quickly showered, put on comfortable clothes, and dug in. "What's the champagne for?" I asked around a mouthful of my favorite shrimp étouffée.

"Our night," my husband responded as if it were obvious. "It's going to be one to remember."

He rarely smiled, but I saw the corner of his mouth twitch, and certain parts of my anatomy sat up at attention. Oh boy, I knew what that meant.

"Kildare," I started.

"Has been dispatched."

Dispatched was a fancy term for terminated. "Thank you, but I could have handled him."

"Of course you could have. But that would have taken time away from our reunion. Besides, I wanted to send a message."

A message to all the supernaturals in the area that his mate was off limits.

"And the bullet?" I asked. "Any idea where that came from?"

"SMG has it. I would love to get my hands on it, but for now, we are in the dark."

A knock came at the door. When Harlow entered with Katarina, Killion's enforcer, I knew they weren't there for a meal. My heart sank.

"We weren't expecting company," my mate said with obvious displeasure.

"I apologize, Master, " Harlow said, eyes averted. "It's important."

My stomach sank even farther. "What is it?"

"Nest business." Katarina swiped a buttermilk biscuit off my plate. "Nothing you need to be part of."

She and I were often at odds, and her goth appearance was no simple makeup trick. She was a one-hundred-percent deadly vampire, and she never let me forget it. Nest business meant vampire business, and not the fun kind involving wine tastings or art auctions.

I held up my glass of champagne in a mock toast to my husband. "Looks like our celebration is about to go off track regardless." Unfortunately, that was nothing new. It seemed we had downtime so rarely anymore. "I do appreciate the effort."

"Quit hovering," Killion ordered Katarina, who was looming over me. "Sit down and tell us what this is about."

She turned a chair around and plunked down, using a serving spoon to scoop out a bite of quiche. "The Aldrichs are missing. Looks like a kidnapping."

The name didn't register, and I kept my mouth shut, except to sip champagne as I studied Killion's reaction.

"Are you sure?" he asked.

Harlow seated herself next to me. At least she had better manners and didn't help herself to my meal. Of course, she might have 'eaten' earlier. Some vampires enjoyed human food, while others stuck to a strict blood diet. "Neither Cormac nor Roma showed up for work, and Rena wasn't at school. They missed the monthly blood donation at the church this evening. They were scheduled to work it."

Killion had a *no-hunting humans* policy. The old, abandoned Catholic church was the place he used for many purposes—training, interrogations of his enemies, and distributing blood supplies to keep the members of his nest from breaking the rules.

Harlow continued. "None of them are answering calls or texts. Katarina and I went to their place and found their front door open. Their dog was in the backyard and had bite marks on it. There was a lot of blood. It belongs to the parents, not the human girl."

I nearly choked. "Their daughter is human?"

"As were they before they were turned," Killion told me. "It's a long story."

Standing in the threshold between the dining room and kitchen, Pennyworth wrung his hands on a dish-towel. "They're from Tiana's group. Is it possible she's come for them?"

Katarina snatched up my glass and downed the rest of the champagne. I curled my lips at her and she returned the expression, hers with some fang thrown in. "Their security system was disabled. Whoever took them knew exactly what they were doing."

"I checked their credit cards, cell phone activity, everything," Harlow said. "There's been nothing since two days ago."

Ghost had left her comfy bed near the fireplace. Sensing my distress, she whined at my feet, and I lifted her into my lap. "Who is Tiana? And what would she want with them?"

Killion, Harlow, and Katarina all glanced at Penny-worth. He stopped twisting the towel. "Tiana is a master vampire in New Orleans. She's called the Blessed Lady by her followers. Humans with severe illnesses or diseases go to her to be turned, and then they become her devoted disciples. One of my friends is in her group."

Killion stared at his empty plate. "Cormac was diag-nosed with multiple sclerosis a few years ago, and as the disease progressed, he and Roma decided to become vampires. They had no other relatives, and Cormac was fading fast. It's not a choice I approve of, but that's what Tiana does. She convinced them they were doing their daughter a favor, and I suspect she would have eventually manipulated them into sacrificing Rena to her as well."

"But they came to us," Katarina said, running one of her painted black nails over the glass stem. "Killion welcomed them to the nest, as long as they agreed to follow our rules. We gave them sanctuary from Tiana and her disciples. Tiana should know better than to touch them. It's grounds for war."

Pennyworth made a snorting noise. "Tiana can't leave New Orleans, but she knows plenty of mercenaries who can. She might keep her distance from unsavory brush-ups with us by using one of them."

Harlow tapped a finger on the table. "She would never cross Killion."

"Never say never." Katarina kicked back in the chair. "I heard through the grapevine that she's growing in numbers. Maybe she's gotten too big for her blessed britches."

I folded my napkin and set it aside. "Where would one of these mercenaries take the family? New Orleans?"

Killion shook his head. "Even if Tiana came after them, it would be to kill them, not kidnap them. I'm not sure we can lay the blame at her feet. We need more intel."

I stood and put Ghost down. "What are we waiting for? I'll ask Andy if he can meet us at their house. Between him and Ghost, they can get the scent of the family, and we can follow the trail."

The temperature in the room dropped several degrees as Killion's gaze locked with mine. "I will handle it. You need to rest."

"The nest is my family, too. I'm going with you."

"This is most likely connected to vampire politics. Old enemies. Blood feuds. You do not need to get involved."

"Or it could be something entirely different," I countered. "And I'm not without skills. I'm part vamp now. I have every right to be part of this."

Corvus, quiet since we'd arrived, croaked from his perch near the window. "Kill!"

In his unique raven language, that was confirmation that he thought I was right. At least, that's what I told myself.

"Chloe..." Killion's tone held a warning.

"You know I can help." I would simply have to keep the exhaustion at bay a while longer. "If something supernatural is involved, we need all hands on deck."

"She's right, Master," Harlow said.

He didn't like that and shot her a glower. She averted her eyes again, and Katarina decided to stay out of what had become a standoff. She poured a fresh glass of champagne and shoved it my way, showing at least a moment of respect.

My husband stood and paced the length of the dining room. The movement was fluid, controlled, reminding me that beneath his expensive suit lay a predator who had survived centuries by being cautious and strategic. "There are others who may be targeting us."

I knew little about vampire politics, and Tiana seemed like a shoo-in to be our bad guy. "Like who?"

Katarina seemed to catch on to what he was thinking. "Hunters? Again, why wouldn't they kill the Aldrichs? Why kidnap them?"

"Why them period?" Harlow added.

"How do you know they haven't been killed?" I hated saying it out loud, but the possibility had to be considered. "They could have kidnapped them and then killed them somewhere else."

All three looked at me with a mix of anger, fear, and contemplation.

"Until we have proof otherwise," Killion said, "we proceed as if they're still alive."

A thought dawned, and I had the eerie sensation that I didn't want to know the answer. Kidnapping meant blackmail, manipulation, a request for ransom money...

Killion stopped in front of me and took my hands. He knew what I was thinking and still wanted to talk me out of helping. "The risk—"

"Is always there." I gave his hands a squeeze. "And I have faced hunters before. With you. Whether I'm crossing spirits who don't want to go or helping you find missing vampires, you and I are my *incatusa sufletum*. We are soulmates. Your fight is my fight."

He stared at me as if he could see straight to my soul. "If anything happened to you..." Then he shook his head. "It would be my fault."

"Nothing's going to happen to me," I promised, though we both knew such guarantees were impossible. "Besides, I have you, Ghost, and Corvus. Not to mention Harlow, Katarina, and a small army of nest members you're bringing into this."

His expression remained grave, but I could sense his resolve weakening. "You are always too bullheaded for your own good."

If that wasn't the vampire calling the grim reaper undead. Ghost pressed against my leg, urging me to stand my ground. "You love me, and you know it," I teased.

Katarina rolled her eyes, rising from her seat and snatching another biscuit. "Death won't like you getting involved, Grave Girl. You're already on his naughty list."

Moss' nickname for me had rubbed off on a few of the other vamps. "What he doesn't know won't hurt him," I said, knowing he would find out and I'd have another problem to deal with. "If he does, I'll handle it."

My bravado masked a more profound certainty. What I was doing was right, even if it complicated my already complicated balance of jobs. Either way, I had to ensure I didn't fail my clinic employees, the animals relying on me, or those who needed my assistance to cross over.

"Andy won't be any help. Harlow and I have already gone over the house in great detail," Katarina said. "We tracked their scent to the driveway, where their door cam shows a large van was parked. Then the footage cuts off, damaged by something, and their scent disappears. I have our best trackers checking traffic cams and other doorbell security cameras in the area."

"I want to have a look at the house myself," I said.

"As do I," Killion replied.

We shared a look, and at that moment, I felt like I was crossing a threshold. I was no longer only balancing all these different aspects of myself but also integrating my roles as healer and reaper, protector of both the living and the dead.

Or the *undead*, in this case.

Ghost's tail thumped against the floor. She was ready to go to work.

5

The moment I stepped through the entrance at the Aldrichs' home, a chill crept across my skin that had nothing to do with their air conditioning. Even Ghost pressed against my calf, her tiny body trembling.

"Easy, girl," I murmured, my grave sight activating. It gave me invisible senses to see, hear, and speak with shades. While vampires rarely fit in that category, it was some relief that I saw none hanging around.

Since becoming a tribrid—part grim, part vampire, and part human—my grave sight had expanded so I could now catch scenes of violence or death. As I scanned the foyer and hall, the world shifted, colors bleeding into grayscale with occasional flashes of energy that morphed between blue and violet.

We fanned out. Ghost's nails clicked on the hardwood as she and I moved into the living room. There was blood splatter and overturned furniture. Killion stayed on my heels, doing his own version of cataloging what his senses told him.

I sorted through the lingering energy imprints to figure out what belonged to the Aldrichs and what belonged to whoever had attacked them. "Do you smell that?" I asked him.

His nostrils flared. "I smell many things, the blood of two vampires, but none of the human daughter. A canine. There's a lingering aroma of metal and wood, possibly from weapons used on them. The other odors are what you would expect in a home—food, cleaning products, shampoo, and soap."

"I get all that, too, but also something earthy, musty, and with a subtle animal quality different from a dog."

"Shifter?"

I shook my head. "Nonliving. There's a chemical mixed in with it." I inhaled again. "Tar, I think."

He frowned, logging the furniture. "Older tanning methods for leather often create a tar-like aroma."

"None of the furniture is leather."

Ghost raised her muzzle, her nose twitching. She bolted from the room. We followed, finding her at the back door with her tail rigid, sniffing at something intently on the floor.

I crouched down. "What did you find?"

"Drool," Harlow told me, emerging from the pantry. "From their dog."

I ran a finger over the crusty residue before bringing it to my nose. The odor was unmistakably canine. Flipping on my cell phone flashlight, I noticed a single short black hair alongside it. I sniffed that as well and examined it in the light. Ghost whined, pawing my wrist.

My mind flashed back to the clinic. "The mastiff," I said.

Everyone looked at me. Katarina strolled in. "What?" she asked.

"A big Neapolitan Mastiff, I think. Black coat, very drool-y. There was one in the clinic this morning with a guy dressed like a cowboy." The duster—tanned leather. I scanned my memory, trying to remember when he'd disappeared. I was sure the dog and the owner had never been seen by any of us in the exam rooms, but in all the chaos, had I missed something? I turned to Killion. "Do you remember him? He was tall and lanky, and his leather duster made him look like he just walked off the set of a spaghetti western. His dog was a huge black mastiff."

My husband shook his head. "The clinic was in chaos. I didn't note any one particular animal or owner."

I peered out the window at the backyard. "What kind of dog do the Aldrichs have?"

Katarina shrugged. "A mix of something with white fur. Terrier and Shepherd, maybe?"

"You said it was injured."

Harlow pointed toward the patio doors that led to a deck. "I healed it from the worst of the wounds, but whatever tore into it was vicious. He probably needs actual medical attention."

"Let me see him."

All of us trooped outside, including Ghost. It was pitch black with the clouds hiding the waning moon, and the back porch light did little to illuminate the yard. Ghost gave a yip, and a pair of eyes appeared behind a set of patio furniture.

I sat and brought out a bag of the bacon-flavored dog treats I kept in my pocket. "Hey, buddy. It's okay. We're not going to hurt you."

I tossed a few of the treats several feet from me and held out another one in my hand. At first, he was skittish and didn't want to leave his hiding place, but the bacon worked its magic, and soon, he crept out and snatched up the closest piece to him. Who can resist bacon?

"Good boy," I said. "Do you think we could get him some water?" I asked Katarina. She huffed and returned to the kitchen.

Harlow sat down next to me and held out her hands, sending her scent his way. "Remember me?"

He eyed her suspiciously but felt confident enough to move forward and grab the next treat. He chewed while keeping watchful eyes on us. He was an interesting mix without a black patch on him. The dog hair was not his.

His fur was stained with blood in places. I wanted to hug and console him, but he was too scared to accept it, and I didn't want to add to his trauma.

"I can put him to sleep," Killion said.

"Absolutely not!" I shot him a horrified look. "Why would you do such a thing?"

"Not in the mortal sense," he said, exasperated. "I meant I could cause him to fall asleep so we can move him to the clinic for proper treatment."

The admonishment in his tone was valid. "Oh, sorry."

I took a deep breath and rubbed my eyes. "It's been a rough one. I'm a bit jumpy."

He crouched next to us, eyeing the dog, but I stopped his hand before he could use his magic to do anything. Ghost was slowly approaching it, tail wagging, and the dog was not growling or backing away. "You may not have to," I said. "Ghost is working her magic."

Using her nose, she nudged one of the treats toward the animal. He sniffed it, sniffed her, and then gulped it down.

It took all the treats I had to coax the dog to come to us. I couldn't exactly examine his wounds in the low light, but I got him to allow me to pet him, and he drank deeply from the bowl of water that Katarina put nearby. After a minute of sweet talk, he sort of folded into my chest.

"You do have a way with animals," Katarina said, "but can we get back to figuring out what happened to the family?"

Gently, I ran my fingers around the dog's collar, finding a metal tag. I didn't want to flash a light in his eyes or startle him, so I had to wait until we got him inside to see what it said. He might also have a chip that I could scan to get details about his age. "I don't think the mastiff's owner filled out the intake form, but I can check. I swear, that hair I found next to the drool is a match."

Harlow frowned. "Were the Aldrichs scheduled to bring this dog in to see you?"

I shook my head. "They're not clients of mine."

"If the cowboy is our culprit and was after them, what's the point of his going to your clinic today?"

Killion gently stroked the dog's ear. "I agree that it's a stretch, but it's a starting point."

"Wait," Harlow said. "Brown hair, about so tall?" She placed a hand at the height of her head. "Did he have a heavy drawl but not native to here?"

"I never heard him speak," I admitted, "Do you know him? I've never seen him before."

She brought out her phone and tapped at the screen. "The man I'm thinking of is Silas Mercer." She showed us a grainy surveillance photo. "He's a hunter from Miami. Bad news. *Really* bad news."

Killion was right—this might not be about Tiana after all.

"Bring the dog," he said, gesturing for us to return inside.

I gently guided the dog off my lap and stood. At first, he seemed reluctant to follow, but Ghost gave him a nudge, and after a few seconds, he ducked his head and strolled through the patio doors.

Inside, he sniffed the air, kept his tail low, and stuck like Velcro to my leg.

Harlow's business-like demeanor slipped to reveal genuine concern. "Mercer hunts supernaturals, but his specialty is vampires. He goes after rogues. Or at least, that was his previous MO. Word is he's moved up to targeting established families. He's into forbidden magic, using it to track and exterminate them."

Katarina snorted. "Great. A wannabe Butch Cassidy with a pet hellhound. I don't suppose you have a theory on why he kidnapped our family rather than killing them?"

Magic. While vampires had plenty of it, my witchy friend Aurora was the expert on the dark stuff. I needed to call her.

Killion was as still as granite, tension radiating from him as he stood near the fireplace. "If he was at the clinic today, he was scouting you," he said without looking at me.

Katarina and Harlow did.

Nothing like being in the spotlight. "And when you showed up, he disappeared," I theorized. A curt nod. "Why me?" I asked, but I already knew the answer.

Katarina ticked reasons off on her fingers. "You're a unique creature whom he wants to gain power from, or he wants to use you to get to the Master for the same reason. Take your pick—it always comes down to power. He could also be working for Tiana, and this is a twofold mission. One, he brings the Aldrichs back to her, and two, he creates a situation where Killion is forced to go to New Orleans to confront her if he wants to enforce his claim on them. If Killion goes there, he's out of his territory, leaving him vulnerable."

Harlow paced. "There is another possibility. Because Mercer toys with magic, he may use them and their blood to power up spells. I'm not sure what he would want the girl for, but if he drains the vampires of blood and then drinks it…"

Katarina made a disgusted sound, somewhere between a hiss and a growl. "Barbaric. I'll string him up and drain *his* blood."

There were plenty of humans and supernaturals willing to use vampire blood to harness similar abilities without the side effects of actually becoming one. The clinical part of my brain that had gotten me through school was already piecing together what a monster like Silas might do with such abilities. What he might do to this poor family. How terrified their daughter must be, no matter what was going on.

I clung to the idea that he might still reach out with a ransom request. The Aldrichs weren't wealthy or politically connected, but not all ransom requests revolved around such things. "So we don't know if this is a ploy to get to me, Killion, or simply a way for Mercer to acquire new magical abilities. I don't care what his endgame is. All that's important at the moment is saving them."

"Chaos creates opportunity," Killion said. "Mercer may be using this as a lead-in to something bigger."

The dog nudged my hand. I found the metal tag and discovered his name. "Redemption," I read out loud. "Interesting."

We split up to search the house, methodically moving through it step by step. Killion took the master bedroom, Harlow the basement, and Katarina the garage. I returned to the kitchen. After finding nothing more there, I searched Rena's bedroom. Redemption stuck close to me, as did Ghost.

The girl had loads of pictures of Redemption on a bulletin board and one on her nightstand. Her favorite color was orange, and she had quite a selection of games and art supplies. She'd painted the dog in many poses and plastered those on her walls.

Redemption whined and hopped up on the bed,

placing his head on his paws and looking at me with sad eyes.

"We're going to get her back," I promised. "Don't worry."

The four of us found no other clues and moved outside to survey the front lawn, sidewalk, and driveway, examining every inch for any sign of a lead. It only led to more dead ends.

Harlow updated us on her research. "Mercer has been spotted with different companions in different cities. Never the same person twice."

"Disposable allies?" Katarina suggested.

"Or test subjects who didn't survive his experiments," Killion suggested.

Raw disgust made my stomach flip. "What about the New Orleans connection?" I asked. "Is there anything directly linking him to Tiana?"

Harlow shook her head. "He did stay there recently for three months. During that time, there was an increase in vampire disappearances. Over a dozen were discovered drained of blood. Another dozen have never been found. I can't believe Tiana or any of the other head vamps would have let Mercer live if he was involved."

"New Orleans is the place of many types of magic," Killion said. "He was most likely using the vampires and the magic to try and hone his skills."

Regardless of my dinner having been interrupted and my stomach being empty, I wanted to vomit. I leaned down and hugged the dog. Redemption accepted it as if it were a balm to his heart.

"Activate our network," Killion said. "Every vampire, every ally we have. I want eyes at every exit from the city."

I'd stuck the dog hair in a plastic bag. I pulled it from my pocket and held it up. "Track the dog. I have the feeling it goes everywhere with him."

Harlow took the bag. "On it." Her fingers flew as she typed on her phone, sending out the word.

Katarina was also sending messages, popping bubbles as she worked over a piece of gum. "We'll find them."

"I need to contact Aurora," I said to Killion. "She might be able to trace this guy's magical signature. Andy's pack can cover ground faster than any of you. It won't hurt to put them on alert and ask for their help with this."

He stared at me and the dog for a long moment. "Why take the girl?" he contemplated out loud. "She's human with no powers."

"Leverage," I said. "I bet she's his backup plan if he needs one."

The three of them considered this, and all the ways the hunter could use Rena if he needed to. I didn't want to think about it, but I knew it was something we had to plan for.

I kissed the top of Redemption's head. "You're coming home with us, buddy," I told him.

"We already have a dog," Killion stated. "I'll find him a temporary foster until we can either bring the family home or—"

"This dog has been through a trauma, and he's now

bonded with me and Ghost." I faced my mate. "He's coming home with us."

Killion opened the telepathic channel between us. *We can't keep collecting strays.*

He's not a stray, and this is non-negotiable.

He'd learned during our time together when not to push me on things. "It's the right thing to do," he announced. His eyes met mine with a light that warmed my insides, despite the awful circumstances. He would make me pay for challenging him later, but in the most delightful way. "Redemption may indeed be useful. He may be the only tracker we need."

I smiled gratefully. "Thank you."

Harlow's phone pinged. "I need to go home and check in with Mason. He's worried. I've warned the rest of the nest to be alert for this bottom feeder. The Aldrichs may not be his only targets."

Killion sent her and Katarina off, and the two of us, plus the dogs, climbed into the limo.

Sunrise was only a few hours away, and I fell asleep with my head on Killion's shoulder. Redemption's head was in my lap, and Ghost's was in his. A made family.

6

"*I* feel so useless," I admitted, voicing the thought that had been plaguing me since the previous night. I'd slept three hours, bedding down in the living room to keep Redemption company. He proved to be equally exhausted, but when I woke to my alarm, I found him freshly bathed, thanks to Pennyworth. I trudged to the dining room. "All my skills and supernatural power, and I can't help find one family."

Killion's voice softened as he moved to stand beside me. "We all feel that way."

With every passing minute, the Aldrichs were probably being taken farther away, and we were no closer to bringing them home.

Pennyworth's partner, Omwee, had taken Redemption and Ghost for a walk in the back gardens behind the hotel. They returned, and Redemption rushed to me as if we'd known each other forever. I hugged him and praised him as Omwee reported that everything had gone as expected. Both dogs inhaled their breakfast while I sat down to do the same.

Omwee was joining the search, and Killion filled him in on what we knew and what he, Katarina, and Harlow were planning. "I have the feeling Mercer didn't go far with an entire family of vampires, even with whatever magic he's using."

Omwee left, and I gathered my things to head to the clinic. I considered taking the day off to help with the search, and since it was Saturday, Megan would be handling the front. Unfortunately, Saturdays were Dr. O'Leary and JR's day off, so I was the only vet on duty, and after yesterday's overabundance of patients, I feared today might still be busy.

Being torn between all the people and animals who needed me was a constant source of stress. While I was getting better at managing it, it still made me reconsider being a grim reaper.

Even if I weren't, I would still be married to a master vampire and part of his nest. Like I told him last night, his family was my family.

My body screamed for more horizontal time. "I need to check in at the clinic and make sure Megan can hold down the fort this morning, then I'll join you to search for the family."

"What you need is rest," Killion said. "Your health is—"

"Non-negotiable, I know," I finished for him. "But so are my responsibilities. This is the best compromise I can offer. Moss can drive me to the clinic, and I can examine Redemption more thoroughly, while helping Megan reschedule patients for next week. When I'm done there, I'll be back."

Killion's ancient eyes scanned me, seeing my determination. *You vex me*, he said mentally.

Good, I retorted.

Finally, he gave a slight nod. "We'll drop you off on the way to the Church."

Once I was ready, I gathered the dogs and Corvus and met Moss downstairs, where he had the limo running. The humidity caused my shirt to cling instantly to my back. "The Smoking Bean, please," I said to him. "I need the biggest caramel mocha latte they could legally sell me, two white chocolate fudge cookies, and whatever pastries will work to bribe my colleagues."

The big man smirked, his suit, a crisp blue. "Whatever, Grave Girl."

Killion followed, and I added, "And coffee for Killion. Black, like his wardrobe and occasionally his mood."

The corner of my husband's mouth twitched. "Not funny."

I held my finger and thumb an inch apart. "A little funny."

Ghost bounded into the backseat, Redemption following with more dignity. Corvus took his preferred seat up front next to Moss. I slid in after the dogs and Killion settled beside me. His mood was black at the moment, and I hoped he didn't feel my teasing was irreverent under the circumstances. As we pulled away, I leaned into him. "You'll find them. I know you will."

He patted my cheek. "I must."

We drove toward coffee, and then my responsibilities,

while Redemption rested his head on my lap. I wondered what he understood about his family's disappearance. More than what we might think, I suspected. Dogs always did.

The sun was already at full strength by the time I stumbled through the clinic doors, and I was grateful for the air-conditioning. Ghost trotted at my heels while Redemption padded along more cautiously, sniffing everything in this unfamiliar territory. My caramel mocha latte was already half empty, and the sugar rush barely put a dent in my exhaustion.

Nita was on the couch in the office, her purple hair in disarray. She yawned as she sat up, arching a brow when she saw Redemption. "Did you get a new dog?"

"Temporary addition." I set the box of pastries on the desk and opened the lid to tempt her. "This is Redemption. He belongs to a family that Killion knows. They're having trouble at the moment, so we're taking care of him for now."

She dove into the pastry box and pulled out a cinnamon and brown sugar scone. "Well, all of your overnight patients are stable. If you want, I'll feed them and take them out to do their business before I leave."

"You're a lifesaver." I offered her one of the coffees I'd also brought.

She accepted it with a smile. "Not gonna lie, you look like death warmed over again. Did Killion not allow you any sleep last night?"

"I was worried about the dog," I said. It wasn't a lie. "I didn't sleep well. How was dinner?"

She nodded while swallowing a bite. "Amazing. And that's all you're getting out of me."

"The two of you weren't doing the nasty in here, where are you?" I teased.

Her expression was wicked. "I never kiss and tell."

While she fed and walked the dogs, I called Aurora and told her what had happened. "I'll be there shortly. Do you need tea?" she asked.

Her teas were awful. "Nope, I've got a latte."

"Those are terrible for you."

"And yet, they work wonders on my attitude. Do you think Andy can come, too? I'd like to fill him in and have him go to the Aldrichs' to see if he can pick up their scent. The vampires tried, but this hunter put the family in a van and drove off. They couldn't follow it."

"He worked all night at Shepherd's Rest again. They've had pranksters causing trouble and two attempts at grave robbing."

"Andy, working a legit job," I mused. "Will wonders never cease?"

"Right? He just got off and is in the shower. I'll bring him along."

We disconnected. I cleaned up some of the mess left from the previous day and was relieved when Megan arrived, wearing her army-green backpack. She wore an oversized T-shirt with hieroglyphics across the front and chunky platform boots. Her latest hairstyle featured a shaved left side, with long, peach-colored strands on the right. Giant cross earrings hung from both ears, and her fingers were decorated with multiple gemstone rings. "Heard you had fun yesterday," she said.

"That's one way to put it. I need you to do me a favor. Any patients today who are scheduled for this afternoon need to be pushed back to next week."

At least she wasn't one to ask a lot of questions. It barely phased her when Redemption appeared and sniffed her pant leg. "New dog alert."

I introduced them, and she dropped her backpack behind the counter. "He's just visiting," I explained.

She bent down and allowed him to explore her hands before she tried to pet him. "Are we closing early?"

"If it's at all possible, yes."

"I can come back around two," Nita said, gathering her things. "I can probably have JR work, too, if you need to bail early and catch some zees."

I rubbed my eyes. "How about if he's on call? No mandatory overtime, but Megan will reach out if someone has an emergency."

She hugged me and stole another pastry. "Try not to fall asleep standing up before then, okay, Morticia?"

The hug and the nickname felt good, normal. There were times I wished I could share all of the supernatural stuff with her, but I needed this connection to the non-magical world. She was my anchor, along with my aunt and uncle. It was better to keep all of them in the dark.

I was finishing up my exam of Redemption when Megan came strolling into the room. "Your first patient isn't supposed to be until nine-thirty, but some lady just showed up with a kitten emergency."

I praised Redemption for being patient and allowing me to check his wounds. They were all healing, and I had given him some antibiotics to make sure they didn't become infected. I went to the sink and washed my hands. "That's fine. Show her to exam room one."

After getting Redemption settled next to the reception desk and seeing how he reacted when Megan fed him a treat from her top drawer, I knew he would be fine without me for a few minutes.

I pushed open the door to the exam room to find a petite woman in a flowing sundress and practical clogs. Light brown hair fell in soft waves around a face that radiated friendliness, and the laugh lines around her eyes confirmed it. In her lap sat a cardboard box, from which tiny mewling sounds emanated.

"Good morning," I said, "I'm Dr. Frost." I would never get tired of saying that. "Who do we have in the box?"

"Sylvie Pearson," she said with a smile. "Me, not the kitten. Just call me Vi. And this little one,"—she opened the lid—"doesn't have a name. I found him under my car this morning, crying his little heart out."

I peered into the box to see a tiny, black kitten, no more than a few weeks old, with one white paw and bright blue eyes. "Poor baby," I cooed, gently lifting him out for examination. My gravesite flickered briefly, showing me the kitten's life force, which was strong and vibrant, but he was hungry. Gently, I listened to his heart and lungs, checked his belly, and inspected his ears.

"He's dehydrated and has a skin rash, possibly from fleas, but seems otherwise okay." Even as I continued my inspection, I couldn't shake the feeling that Ms. Pearson was studying me as carefully as I was examining my patient. "Looks like you've been adopted," I told her.

She smiled. "Oh, I was hoping you knew of a rescue, or maybe you would take him?"

The rescues and shelters overflowed with kittens this time of year. None of them could take more. "I'm sure I can arrange something, but trust me, this kitten has chosen you. They have a way of finding exactly who they need."

"Kind of like how certain souls find their reaper?"

I froze, my fingers stopping mid-stroke of the kitten's belly where the rash was focused. "Excuse me?"

Her expression remained open and curious, no hint of anything suspicious. "Oh, I just repeated what you said —cats find their owners," she replied smoothly. "That is what you said, right?"

I blinked, suddenly questioning what I'd heard. My lack of sleep was making me hallucinate. "Yes, that's what I've learned as a vet."

I finished the exam, showing her how to bottle-feed the kitten while explaining what supplies she needed. "I'm somewhat familiar with the process," she assured me.

All the while, I continued to have the nagging sensation that there was more to this woman than met the eye.

Was I being paranoid after the night chasing Silas Mercer? I chalked it up to that as I walked her and her new kitten to the front. Megan set her up for her next appointment and handed her my card.

"This is such a lovely clinic," Ms. Pearson said. "My last job before I moved here was as office manager for a big clinic in Baton Rouge. I like the vibe you have here better."

I nearly choked. "You were an office manager at a vet clinic?"

She nodded. "I love animals."

Megan shot me a look. "Serendipity. We have an opening for a full-time manager."

The woman's smile widened. "You do? Are you taking applications?"

Before I could react, Megan whipped out our form. "How soon can you start?"

"Now, wait a minute," I said. "Ms. Pearson can fill out the application, and we'll get back to her."

Megan gave me her flat, *are you kidding me* look. "Do you want a repeat of yesterday come Monday?"

"It's Vi, please. What happened yesterday?" she asked.

"Nothing," I said, a warning in my voice to Megan. "Fill out the form, and then we'll schedule an interview."

"Lovely." Her grin now took up half her face. "I'll be back," she said, waving the business card at me. "Have a great day, Dr. Frost."

"What just happened?" I asked, more to myself than to Megan.

Corvus squawked. Megan rolled her eyes. "Like I said, serendipity. She's perfect for the job."

"We don't even know her."

"The universe sent her to you. Don't be stupid."

I cocked a brow.

"Sorry," she said, not sounding sorry at all. "It's just that you overthink everything. You act like everybody is suspicious and out to get you. Newsflash. Not everything's about you."

I really should fire her.

7

I wore a path in the floor of the Catholic church on Sunday afternoon. The building and grounds were considered a place between this reality and an invisible realm. Although most humans could see the place, the glamours infused into the stones, the parking lot, and the graveyard kept them from truly *seeing* it. The wards encouraged the curious to move along, look the other way, and forget it even existed once they had passed by.

It was now our command center. The pews had been moved to the sides in the nave, and a temporary station was set up with computers and other equipment. A dozen vampires, along with Andy and another dozen of his pack, worked side-by-side as Killion issued orders and established teams to sweep the town. None had been able to track Mercer, nor his dog. I had attempted to get Redemption and Ghost to track the Aldrichs, based on the scent of some of their clothing, but even that had failed.

Two days. They'd been missing for forty-eight hours, and we had nothing to show for our search efforts so far.

"If you pace any faster, you might actually time travel," Andy teased, not turning from his position near Harlow, who was seated at the main desk, watching video feeds from traffic cams. A few of them had picked up the van, but it appeared it had never left town.

"Very funny," I muttered. "I'm just trying to think."

"I can hear your thoughts from here," Killion said. His silhouette cut a stark figure in front of one of the floor-to-ceiling stained glass windows. "They are loud and chaotic."

That was my mate's way of saying, 'You're driving me crazy, but I'm too polite to say it directly.' It was so natural these days to share our telepathy that most of the time, I didn't bother putting up barriers. Right now, my mental and emotional world probably felt like a tornado in his head.

"I can't help it," I said, stopping to stare out the window with him. "Every one of our ideas has failed. I've failed."

"We all take responsibility for this," he said. His intense and determined gaze settled on me, and my pulse skipped in response. I was grateful for the more satisfying reunion we'd enjoyed the previous night and the fact that I'd gotten more sleep. Once we found the family, there would be time for more of both, but it didn't lessen the ache inside me for his touch.

Not the time, I reprimanded myself, even as I instinctively moved closer to him.

The others must have felt the sexual energy snap

between us. Several people straightened, others cleared their throats, and hustled farther away. "Sorry," I whispered to him. "I can't seem to help that either."

He drew me close and kissed me. "Never apologize for our connection."

Aurora's cherry red curls fell forward as she traced a line on one of her maps. The triquetra tattoo on her wrist was visible beneath layers of bangle bracelets. Andy sat across from her at the large conference table, currently buried under an avalanche of papers, magical texts, and every survey map of the city.

"This ley line intersects with a crossroads," she said. "If Mercer is using blood magic to hide himself and the vampires, he needs a power source to keep the spell at full force. This natural energy spot may work for him."

"Have you tried scrying again?" I asked, pulling away from Killion to join her and Andy.

She glanced up, her emerald eyes tired but hopeful. "Three times already this morning. I'm beginning to think he's not here anymore, even though the traffic cams didn't pick him up. That he took them and bailed."

Andy nodded. "Maybe he transferred them to a different vehicle."

"There is only one rental place in town, and they've had no clients in a week," Harlow insisted. "The police report no stolen vehicles. He has not vanished into thin air, nor left the city limits. He's hiding."

Killion strode to the conference table. "She's right. Silas Mercer is still human, even if he's using magic for power and protection. Still mortal. Perhaps we need to think like a mortal."

Aurora glanced toward a stack of her books. "Andy, hand me the grimoire of shadows."

He passed her a volume that appeared to predate the printing press. Its leather binding was cracked with age. She flipped through the fragile pages with practiced care.

"What is it?" I asked.

"Even if he's using magic, hiding three people plus himself requires a landing spot. What Harlow and Killion said is right. He can't disappear into thin air, and he can't move them around easily. If he's using the ley line-crossroad intersection, there must be an abandoned or empty building nearby that he can draw that power into. And every bit of that power leaves a magical trace. One I can locate and follow."

Now we were getting somewhere.

The floor beneath us rippled like a stone had been tossed into a pond, and the air pressure dropped so suddenly my ears popped. Ghost, who had been napping on the floor, shot to her feet with her fur standing on end. Redemption, who had been watching me pace, also came to attention, both staring at a vortex of shadows that materialized on the dais.

"Knock, knock," boomed a voice that seemed to come from everywhere and nowhere at once. Death stepped out of the shadows, dressed in cargo pants, a hoodie, and combat boots. He took in the room and all the supernaturals, most staring wide-eyed at him.

It was rare for him to allow anyone to see him, but today, no one could miss his giant frame as he set his hands on his hips. "Having a party, Fang Boy, and you didn't invite me?"

"Who ordered the harbinger of doom?" Andy muttered under his breath.

"No party," Killion said on a snarl. He hated Death's irreverent nickname. "Three members of my nest are missing. We are searching for them."

Death's black hair cascaded to his shoulders, and frosty grey-green eyes surveyed the room again. Disgust showed on his face. He hated vampires because he believed they had cheated him by becoming Undead. Every muscle seemed to flex simultaneously, as if his physical form could barely contain the primal power within. "Are you sure they want to be found?"

I glanced at Killion. We hadn't considered any option other than that the family had been taken by force. "There is blood at the scene, and everything was trashed, suggesting they didn't leave on their own accord," I told him.

"Did they have enemies?" he asked.

"None that we're aware of, "Killion replied.

Death shrugged and hopped down from the stage. "I've been looking all over for you," he said to me. "Your signal is wonky."

"My signal?"

He glanced at Killion. "Are you testing new glamours on her?"

My husband narrowed his eyes. "If only she would let me."

The two of them were only a few feet apart, and although they'd been working together to gather the Wild Hunt members, their animosity was always brewing right under the surface. I stepped between them. "You found me," I said to my boss, making a mental note to ask Killion later if he *had* placed some sort of new ward on me without telling me. "I apologize that I couldn't drop what I was doing Friday and take care of those souls, but Ghost and Corvus handled it. If you came here to reprimand me—"

Death produced a small scroll tied with a black ribbon and handed it to me. "I've already written you up about Friday. This is your new assignment." He tossed it at me, and I barely caught it.

Familiar tingles of magic raced over my fingertips and up to my skull and crossbones tattoo. "We are kind of in the middle of something," I said, trying to return it to him.

"Aren't we all?" He crossed his arms over his massive chest. "The universe doesn't stop turning because a few vampires went missing. You'll want this assignment. Trust me."

The gall of this guy. "They're part of Killion's family— my family, now—and their daughter is still human. Why don't you lend us a hand so we can find them, and then I'll be all yours to reap whoever you want?"

"Take the assignment," he ordered, and his power vibrated in my bones.

For all intents and purposes, he was a boss I could not deny, no matter how hard I wanted to. I unrolled the scroll, and when I saw the name on it, my heart nearly stopped.

"Silas Mercer?" I glanced up at him, not bothering to hide my shock. "That's who we're hunting. We believe he kidnapped the family."

"The very same guy," he confirmed. "His contract was up six months ago, and because of the magic he's been dabbling in, he's avoided it. None of my other reapers have been able to find him, so guess what? He's here in Danté's Grove, and you're available."

"You're sure he's here?"

A nod.

Harlow began typing furiously. "I knew it."

"But technically, he's human," I said. I was always given the supernatural noncompliants. "You're giving me a mortal to reap?"

Killion took the scroll from my hand to examine it. "Can you assist us in locating him? If we find him, we can find out where the missing family is."

"He's violated too many natural laws," Death said to me. "The scales need balancing."

The universe was big on that, although there had been many instances I'd witnessed since becoming a grim reaper where it seemed things were getting more unbalanced by the day. "And you can help us find him, right?"

Death shook his head. "This assignment is all on you. But I can tell you this: because of the blood magic he's using, he can shift between the living world and the dead one, just like you. His essence lies in a liminal space, akin to the Ghost Lands. That creates an invisibility wall that shields him from the sight of reapers, as well as me. Because of your...enhanced abilities, and the fact that we believe he's here searching for a way to harness those abilities, you may be the only person who can locate him."

"That explains why we haven't been able to track him," Katarina piped up.

"And why my locator spells keep failing," Aurora added.

Andy sat back, shaking his head. "And why I can't catch his scent."

Killion crumpled the paper. "What do you mean he's searching for a way to use Chloe's abilities?"

"Like most of the supernatural world, he's heard that she's the original grim and has necromantic skills." Death fiddled inside one of the pockets in his cargo pants and handed me a tiny metal cross. "Like so many others, he thinks he's found a way to use you to further his objectives."

Although we'd already considered that fact, Killion's protective magic wrapped an extra layer around me. He shifted even closer to my side. "Which are?"

"To avoid being reaped, mate," Death said, always playing around with accents as much as his hair color. He favored his Aussie one. "He's afraid of what waits for him on the other side, and rightfully so."

"What's this?" I asked, taking the charm.

Death pointed at the piece of metal. "It belonged to his wife a long time ago. You may be able to use it with your psychometry to locate him."

I nervously traced the edges of the cross, worried I might get a hit that showed me more than I wanted. Psychometry was a peculiar phenomenon, and on several occasions, I had been unexpectedly projected through time and space.

Ghost sniffed the air at my feet. Nothing happened, though. I shook my head. "I'm not getting anything."

Death sighed dramatically. "Well, it was worth a try. Looks like you're going to have to walk between realms to find him. Bottom line, reaping him takes precedence over finding the blood suckers."

"I'm going to find the Aldrichs," I insisted, "and I'll happily reap Mercer after I do."

Death drew up to his full height. "You're already on thin ice with Smudgy. While you are a valuable employee, they have overlooked an incredible amount of code-breaking and insubordination. For once, can you fulfill an assignment without creating trouble? If you don't, you'll find Internal Affairs breathing down your neck."

"I didn't know we had an internal affairs department." I was less concerned about them than I was about Mei Han, the head of Soul Management Group. Whenever I had to negotiate with Mei, I felt like I was losing a piece of my soul. "I'll do my best." It was all I could promise.

Death clapped his hands together. "Got a tsunami to attend to. The paperwork is a nightmare." With that, he blinked out in a puff of swirling shadows.

"You have to hand it to him," Andy said. "He knows how to make an exit."

Killion's hand tightened on my shoulder, spinning me to face him. His violet eyes took on a slight crimson glow, a sign that he was upset. "You are not crossing dimensions to hunt Mercer. You're also not going to reap him until he tells us where the Aldrichs are."

I bristled at his tone. "I may not be able to find them unless I do."

"He may be too strong to fight there. We need a way to bring him fully into this realm, and if he's taken the family to the in-between..."

They might not survive if we were to bring them back. My stomach fell, and my heart squeezed. "It's our only option at the moment. I'm a reaper, and a good one. This is what I do. Let me do it. You know the Aldrichs are still my priority, but if I find Mercer, I will likely find them as well. Two birds, one scythe."

His grip tightened. "Even the most powerful beings who've entered the land of the dead and wandered there too long have forgotten their connection to the living."

He didn't have to remind me.

Aurora cleared her throat. "We can arm Chloe with enchantments that can help keep her tethered here."

Killion shook his head, continuing to mind-meld me. "Until we have more information and can ensure your safety, I am asking you not to cross the veil."

Part of me wanted to remind him that I was a grown woman who had been reaping souls for over a year. The concern in his eyes stopped me. This wasn't about control; it was about fear. He had a real, genuine fear of losing me.

"A compromise," I said. "I can peek into the in-between—just briefly—without fully crossing over. That might at least give us a sense of Mercer's direction. I might even be able to see through the veil of his invisibility cloak to find where the family is hidden."

Aurora brought over a text, flipping the pages to the

one she wanted. "I've been researching liminal spaces. There are specific locations, including the crossroads, where you can safely glimpse the other side while still fully tethered here."

Killion frowned. "For how long?"

"Minutes," Aurora said firmly. "More than five, but less than ten, if I'm deciphering this correctly. We can set a timer, perform a tethering spell to reinforce her connection, and if all of us are gathered at the crossroads with her, we can pull her back if needed."

Andy got to his feet and sauntered over. "Wolf senses might pick up something if the guy is nearby in the real world. Your vamps might also be able to tap into it through Chloe's connection."

Killion gripped my hand and squeezed. Now *his* thoughts were a tornado, and I caught many of them, understanding what a predicament he was in. He wanted to save the Aldrichs with every fiber in his being, and he also wanted to keep me safe. The two things were at war with each other, and I tried to soothe him. *This could work. I can fulfill my duty to Death while keeping my promise to you. It's worth a try.*

His eyes met mine, an ocean of centuries-old wisdom unable to cover up his vulnerability. "I will be your anchor."

My heart fluttered again. "That's all I need."

My phone rang, the sound too sharp and out of place in the tense silence surrounding us. I grabbed it from my pocket to see JR's number. "Hey," I answered. "Today's your day off, remember?"

"I found our new office manager," he said, excitedly.

"Her name is Sylvie Pearson. She was at church this morning, and she and Mom hit it off. I can't believe our luck, Chloe! She's perfect. I told her to come by this afternoon at three for an interview. Do you want me to handle it, or can you? She can start tomorrow, first thing."

Ugh. "I've met her." Either the universe was shoving this woman at me for a reason, or something more nefarious was going on. Either way, I needed to know what it was. "I'll handle the interview."

We disconnected, and I gave a brief exclamation to the questioning looks surrounding me. "I need to do an interview for the office manager position at the clinic, and then I'll be ready to hit the crossroads, all right?"

"Do you have to do that right now?" Harlow asked with shock.

"I get it. We've got a missing vampire family, a supernatural hunter on the loose, and Death breathing down my neck, but sure, let's interview for an office manager position." I took a deep breath. "But here's the thing. This will allow me more time to focus and concentrate on Mercer and the Aldrichs."

Killion frowned again, but nodded. "The less stress you have before you tackle the in-between, the better. Moss will take you to the clinic."

I kissed his cheek. "Thank you."

"I'll go with you," Aurora volunteered. "I'll work on the tethering spell on the way."

"I might as well go, too," Andy said.

Killion assigned three of his vampires, including Katarina, to accompany me. It was sheer overkill, and I'd have to keep them out of sight so they didn't frighten Sylvie off, but I didn't argue.

Be safe, Killion said through our link as I turned for the exit. *If the hunter's ultimate goal is to snatch you—*

He'll get a rude surprise, I replied. *I'll be ready for him.*

Ghost and Redemption followed, and my new pack of bodyguards and I went to hire an office manager.

If that's all she was...

8

_T_he quiet of the clinic felt almost eerie after the past few days of mayhem. I often looked forward to coming in on Sundays because I could piddle around restocking ear swabs and cotton balls, while feeling my parents' presence in every room.

They'd died in a car accident when I was eighteen. I'd only recently learned that I had died too, but my inherent necromancy as Grim Zero—the original grim—had managed to bring me back to life. I still felt guilty for surviving the accident, and wished I had known then what I do now. Perhaps I would have been able to save them, too.

Their life contracts had been up, though. In some ways, I was glad they'd moved to the afterlife together, where they could hang out with animals and each other forever.

Today, there were no barking dogs, hissing cats, or exotic pet owners insisting their iguana was just feeling blue. We rarely had weekend occupants in the kennels, and I had been able to send both of our overnight guests home the previous day.

This visit wasn't entirely peaceful, though. I had a squad with me and needed to prep for Sylvie's interview. Aurora was in the break room with Andy. Moss was waiting in the limo, and two of Killion's bodyguards were keeping eyes on the front and back doors. I had no idea where Katarina had disappeared to, but I knew she was close by.

Killion excelled significantly more at the business side of things than I did. Give me an animal to treat, and I'm in my glory. Paperwork, forms, interviews... Admin isn't my jam. That's why I needed a competent office manager who could handle appointments, ringing phones, and filing, while still enjoying the hectic pace.

It was a tall order, and I knew Megan and JR were right about accepting this boon with Sylvie.

The bell above the door jingled, and I straightened in the office chair, plastering on a smile. "Hi, there, Ms. Pearson."

She held the kitten in one hand, tucked against her dress. A large tote hung from her shoulder, and he extended her empty hand. "Please, call me Vi."

Her handshake was firm, and her hand felt normal. There was no magical zap or other sensation suggesting she was supernatural. She seemed completely human. "Let's go back to my office."

She followed me down the hall. "I've learned that Frosty Paws has a wonderful reputation in the community." Ghost came barreling out of the back, and Vi stopped momentarily to greet her. "Well, hello there, pretty girl."

"That's Ghost," I said, watching my psychopomp instantly warm to the woman. "She tends to hang out with me as much as possible. Corvus, my raven does, too, but I left him at home this morning."

"A raven is such a cool pet."

I ushered her inside and closed the door. "Have you named your new family member?"

She tucked the sleeping kitten into her lap. "Not yet. I want to get to know his personality before I do."

Ghost hopped up on the sofa, watching Vi. "That's a great idea," I said, grabbing a tablet and pen. "Did you fill out the application?"

She rummaged in her bag. "I've got it right here. Also,"—she handed me the form with an extra sheet of paper—"here are my references."

I glanced over both. "Why did you move to Danté's Grove?"

"Baton Rouge has become crowded—too big city for me. I'm looking for a gentler life. Small town, a real community." She sat forward, handing me yet another paper. "I brought some samples of organizational systems I implemented at my previous job. Also, there's my certification in veterinary office management."

I looked over the impressively color-coded schedules and filing systems, feeling my anxiety ease. "You like spreadsheets?"

"Love them. I designed a system that automatically flags when vaccinations are due, generates reminders and emails, and color codes by urgency." She edged closer to the desk. "And that's the inventory management setup I created. It reduced ordering errors by sixty percent, saving my last clinic nearly five thousand dollars annually."

I let out a low whistle. "That's impressive."

She laughed. "I'm a bit of an organizational nerd. My ex used to say I could probably organize a hurricane if given enough sticky notes and file folders."

"You're exactly the kind of nerd this place needs." I had to admit it to myself as well as her. "How's your experience with different animal species? Exotics? Farm animals?"

She brightened even more. "I've handled everything from parakeets to pot-bellied pigs. Last year, I assisted in the rehabilitation of a red-tailed hawk with a broken wing. Beautiful creatures. Ravens have always been favorites. Such intelligence in their eyes, don't you think?"

Ghost yipped.

Vi gave another of those soft laughs. "And of course Papillon mixes."

"Good guess. One of these days, I'm going to do a DNA swab on her and find out what the rest is." I shifted the stack of her papers aside. "What about difficult clients?" I asked. "We get some interesting personalities here."

"You mean the owners who do an internet search for symptoms at midnight and come in convinced their perfectly healthy goldfish has tuberculosis?" She waved a hand through the air. "I work hard at the gentle art of client education. Kill him with kindness, that's my motto."

She was perfect. Too perfect. "You do seem to know exactly what you're getting into."

"I've been in the veterinary field for fifteen years as an office assistant. I've seen everything from emotional support alligators to cats who supposedly only speak French." She flashed that brilliant smile. "What I love about this work is that every quirky owner cares deeply about their pet. I'll always be supportive of that."

I could find no fault with her. Was I being too paranoid? She was human, and she loved animals. She was organized and had a thing for spreadsheets.

With everything going sideways in my supernatural life, maybe adding some competence to my normal one wasn't a terrible idea.

Plus, I could always fire her.

"So," Vi said, "when would you need me to start?"

"Yesterday, if I'm being honest. My previous office manager eloped. I'm warning you that her shoes will be hard to fill, but with all your experience, I think you'll do just fine."

"Dr. Banks told me this morning at church that you reopened this clinic recently. He mentioned your folks' passing. I'm so sorry."

The old grief rose in my chest, and I forced a smile to cover it. "I appreciate that. This clinic was theirs, and it sat empty for years. It has always been my dream to reopen it, and now I have. This town needs us."

The kitten stirred in her lap, and she cooed at it, stroking its back. "I'm sure they're proud of you."

I reshuffled her paperwork. I liked hearing that, but it always made me feel weird, nevertheless. "One last question. There are times when unexpected situations arise.

The kind that requires me to leave without much notice. Can you handle that?"

She tilted her head. "You mean like family emergencies?"

Something like that. "I occasionally have obligations requiring me to respond immediately. Most days, there are two vets here, if not all three of us, so it's not as if you'll be all on your own, but it may throw a wrench in the appointment book."

"I can hold down the fort when that happens."

I rattled off the hours, salary, and the few benefits I could offer. She seemed pleased. "Do you have any questions for me?" I asked.

"Will you at least give me a week to prove myself?"

"Like a probationary period?"

She nodded. "It will put your mind at ease."

What was there left to say? "Well," I said, standing. "You start tomorrow for your probationary period."

Rising with the kitten in hand, she practically bobbed on her toes with joy as she hooked her bag strap over her shoulder. "Wonderful! I'm thrilled you're giving me a chance."

"I'll have all the paperwork ready for you tomorrow morning and walk you through our system. Could you come at seven thirty so we have time to get you up to speed before our first patient arrives at nine?"

"Can I bring the kitten?"

"Of course."

She paused at the clinic exit and patted my arm. "Don't worry about a thing. I catch on quick. You focus on whatever's keeping you up at night, and I'll handle things here."

The door closed behind her before I could respond.

"There's something off about her," I mumbled to myself.

"She's human. They're all weirdos," Katarina replied from behind me.

Startled, I whirled to face her. "Did you get any supernatural vibes off her?"

She quirked her lips and sucked on a tooth. "She's as mundane as they come."

Hmm.

9

The sky had faded to a dusky violet when I pushed through the penthouse door, Ghost and Redemption with me.

My bones felt like hundred-pound weights, my mind turning with thoughts of Sylvie, Silas Mercer, and what awaited me at the crossroads.

"I'm home," I called, my voice echoing through the living area.

The dogs went to their beds to make themselves comfortable, and Killion materialized from his office. He was still dressed in all black, ready for our adventure. "I take it the interview went well?" His deep, comforting voice made even the most mundane questions sound like poetry.

"I just hired the receptionist of the century, or at least one very polite mundane who's hiding the secret of the century. Stay tuned for further details."

He rubbed the back of my skull and neck, releasing

some of the tension stuck there. "What is it about her that bothers you?"

"Technically speaking, she's perfect for the clinic. That may be what has my Spidey senses tingling. No one is that perfect." I moaned under his ministrations, and brightened at the fact that Pennyworth had cooked. The smell of my favorite quiche tickled my nose and made my stomach growl. "But that's a problem for Monday Chloe. Tonight, reaper Chloe has a supernatural hunter to find."

Killion kissed my temple and drew me to the dining table. Andy and Aurora were already there, having taken her car and left the clinic an hour before I did. She looked up from her spot at the far end of the table, where she ate roasted meat and veggies as she consulted her books. Some pages were marked with glowing, sticky notes, and I could see where she highlighted certain sections. "Good. You're finally back. Twilight is the best time for us to try this."

"We've been researching methods to help you put a tracker on Mercer if you can get close enough to him," Andy said. He, too, was feeding himself, speaking around bites. "And we've created the anchoring spell. It will be temporary, but it's super powerful."

Aurora closed her text, wiped her hands, and stood. "It's like rappelling down a cliff." She motioned at him to finish so we could get going. "You go into the space, but we're holding the rope, and we can haul you out if you get into trouble."

My hopes of feasting on the meal in front of me died. I stared at the quiche and fresh bread with longing. "It's a metaphysical rope, right? I can take my scythe and Ghost, but I can't be wandering the spirit realm with actual climbing gear."

The two gathered the books and maps, stuffing them into a large tote before heading for the exit. "Metaphysical, of course," Aurora clarified.

Andy grinned. "Although the mental image of you hunting that guy in a harness and helmet is rather funny."

Pennyworth appeared from the kitchen at that moment, carrying a to-go cup and a covered container. He shoved both into my hands. "You can eat on the way. No sense taking on such evil on an empty stomach."

"Bless you," I said, sipping from the cup. A strong iced tea, sweetened with plenty of sugar, cooled my over-heated body. I wished I could stay in the penthouse's air conditioning rather than the heat and humidity waiting for me outside.

Ghost recognized that we were going on an adventure and hopped up from her bed. Redemption only curled tighter into herself, and it seemed a better idea for her to stay behind.

All through town, Killion was particularly quiet, and I was busy shoveling food into my mouth to make conversation. Mostly, I listened to Aurora explain the anchoring spell and the tracker.

I should have expected where the crossroads would be, but when we pulled up to Shepherd's Rest, I felt a new level of tension prickle my spine. "You're kidding. This is where we're doing it?"

The entire cemetery was a run-down shell of what it

had once been. The church had long ago been reduced to its foundation stones by a fire.

"My home away from home these days," Andy smirked. "My new job has been enlightening, to say the least. See any ghosts?"

The dead who lingered ducked behind elaborate gravestones, mausoleums, and angel statues as I emerged from the backseat. "Just a few."

"We're not here for them," Killion reminded me. Weak rays of the sinking sun caught in his blue black hair and disappeared, the color so rich it soaked them up. "Let's get on with it."

I was surprised he was in such a hurry to send me to the in-between. I'd gone hunting there before when I didn't know what I was doing and was attacked by violent spirits who'd been stuck there thanks to an evil sorcerer. The Ghost Lands, as they were typically called, were no joke, but there was more to the layers of in-between than just them. Unfortunately, I had no idea how much more. It was like sailing an ocean but only being able to see a few feet in front of you. Nothing worked there like it did on this plane—not gravity or physics. Not even my death blade, sometimes.

I drew the scythe from my bag anyway. It was as much a part of me as my tattoo and blue-green eyes. "Explain the plan to me. What are you going to be doing on this end?"

"We'll be here the entire time, holding you steady." Aurora handed me a plump leather bag, the ties of which glowed green. Her tattoo glowed the same color. "The spell creates a tether between your essence and ours.

Everything inside here has been charmed to boost your powers."

"Yeah, like in Destiny 2," Andy added. We all looked at him with blank expressions. "Come on, guys. You need to up your gaming." He switched his focus to me. "The artifacts will amplify your power, give you extended health, and unlock perks."

"Perks?" I asked.

"Remember how the last time we went into that realm, the gravity was wonky for us?"

I nodded.

He pointed at the bag. "The blue crystal will give you balance."

"The feather enhances your voice commands," Aurora added. "And the string of beads will create a sort of lasso if you need to capture anything. Oh, and the pushpin—when you locate Mercer's imprint signature, stick that in it. It will cause a marker to show up on my map." She held up a piece of parchment.

"Perks," Andy repeated. "Get it?"

"Normal girls get smooth skin or thick eyelashes. I get magical crystals and feathers."

"And me," Killion said, touching my back. "And I am, under most circumstances and in most dimensions, a definite perk."

I smiled and dropped a kiss on his cheek. "That you are, but there's no need for you to go in with me. I can handle this." I pocketed the leather bag, hoping I wouldn't need any of the items. "It's only a sneak and peek. I'm not going to confront rogue hunters or cross over lost souls."

"I'm still attending you," he said.

Sometimes his antiquated lexicon was cute. At other times, it made me question my comprehension. "Attending me?"

"Assisting."

"*Protecting*," I clarified, "because you're worried I can't handle it on my own in the interdimensional wasteland where souls get trapped, and yet, I'm the grim. I deal with death and lost souls every day."

Andy and Aurora did their best to look preoccupied with the nearest above-ground crypt as Killion and I engaged in a trademark staring contest. Neither of us would give an inch.

After several seconds, he exhaled audibly to signify his surrender. Sort of. Vampires don't need to breathe, so it was for dramatic effect, and he never conceded. Not really. "Where you go, I go," he said. "If you are offended by the fact that I feel the need to keep you safe, as always, it is noted and respected, but it will not stop me from crossing into the Ghost Lands with you. Ghost will take us in and carry us out. She's done so before and can again."

My psychopomp barked and morphed into her hulking, monstrous form.

"Killion..." I tried to find a more commanding tone. Truth was, I had no valid argument to keep him from going with me outside of my own annoyance that he wanted to babysit me. On our previous excursion, he'd fared better than I had. "I need you in this plane to tether me."

"I was going to suggest the same," Aurora added.

"With your connection, you can feed the tether on this end and strengthen it far more than any of my spells."

I could see him turning it over in his head, even though I couldn't hear his thoughts. He was keeping them from me, but that was logic he couldn't deny.

"You will follow our safety protocols to the letter," he told me in his commanding, master vampire tone. It made the blood in my bones vibrate, as if he could physically force me to do his will. "No improvising. No going off script."

I swallowed hard and cleared my throat, trying to shake off the command. He rarely used it with me, which meant he was genuinely concerned. After all the things we had been through together, and the fact that I carried his unique dragon blood, this spoke volumes. Because of what had happened in his Romanian castle, he didn't even trust his own magic these days.

I did an impression of Diego's finger salute. "Scout's honor."

"You were never a scout," he said. "And you've promised many things before, and then went back on them when one of us was in trouble."

"And it's a good thing I did," I snapped. "Otherwise, you might not be here."

"We're losing twilight," Aurora griped, beginning to prep the ritual space in the crossroads between the path leading to the former church and the long-ago abandoned road that bisected it from the cemetery. Candles, dried herbs and flowers, and a picture of my parents were placed in the circle.

"Is that the photo from my desk at work?"

She straightened and dug out a lighter, handing it to Andy to begin lighting the candles. "I'm going to call on their spirits to help with the tethering spell. Between them and Killion, along with my enchantment, there's no way you'll get stuck in the interdimensional wasteland."

My insides warred with my increasing worry as I glanced at the three of them. Three members of my supernatural family were ready to hold my lifeline while I walked through a domain that Death himself avoided. Summoning my courage, I pasted on a confident smile. "I've got a soul to find and a family to save." As I moved into the center of the ritual space, I felt the distance between myself and them grow and expand. Aurora began chanting the spell, and a thread of magic wound its way into my chest.

Andy and Killion took up spots at the north and south points, adding their enhanced powers to the thread. It became thicker, stronger, and braided fibers into the binding Aurora was creating.

Ghost entered the circle. Beneath my feet, I felt the ley line light up with a frigid intensity. It rose through my legs and tangled with the tether anchored in my chest. Closing my eyes and sinking one hand into Ghost's mane, I gripped my scythe tightly with the other hand. My grave sight activated in full force and locked onto the tether. At the same time, the veil between worlds thinned.

The souls lingering in the graveyard peeked out from behind their hiding places, drawn to my energy as I crossed into the other world. They couldn't help it— while they feared moving on, it was like a magnet, pulling them in.

But I didn't have time to move them into the afterlife, so I raised my blade and flashed it at them, sending them scattering back to their hidey holes.

Sending love down our channel to Killion, I released my last grip on my physical body. I became lighter, as light as the feather in the leather bag, and my astral self felt the heat of my grim tattoo as it came to life.

With Ghost transporting me through the veil, we left the earth's time and space and stepped through the portal into the in-between.

$\mathcal{I}$t felt like plunging into an ice bath while wrapped in lightning bolts. One second, I stood in Shepherd's Rest Cemetery, my friends' anxious faces surrounding me, and the next I was...

Elsewhere.

When I died and entered this plane, it was easier. When my body was physically alive, not so much. A thousand pin pricks covered my skin. My breath clouded in front of me, as if it were winter here. The in-between stretched before me in a monochrome palette of gray and white as if someone had sucked all the color from the world and left only shadows.

Familiar landmarks from the cemetery, including headstones, trees, and the wrought iron fence, all appeared as blurred echoes of themselves. "The travel brochure oversold the ambience," I murmured, more due to nerves than anything.

Ghost snorted beside me. She knew the stakes as well as I did.

"We've got this, right?"

The bone-deep chill seeped through my clothes, the cold invasive enough to freeze my soul. I drew my jacket tighter, though I knew it was more a matter of psychological comfort than actual protection.

Closing my eyes, I concentrated on the silver threads connecting me to the physical world where Killion, Aurora, and Andy maintained my anchor. The master vampire's centuries of power, Aurora's witchcraft, and Andy's shifter energy combined to create a lifeline that reassured me. I couldn't sense my parents, but I hoped Aurora had managed to draw them into the circle enough to add their love to the grounding ties.

The air tasted like dust and electrified fog. I gripped my scythe tighter and took a tentative step forward, testing the gravity.

While the ground felt spongy, I stayed upright and didn't feel drunk like I had on my previous visit. Maybe the blue crystal was working.

Ghost and I continued onward as I studied the geography. The landscape grew increasingly unfamiliar, but the feel of it did not. The cemetery faded, replaced by twisted terrain that bore no resemblance to earthly topography. I sent out teasers of my magic, trying to find some pulse to indicate where Silas Mercer was hiding.

That's when I saw them—the first of the trapped souls.

They flickered like damaged projections, their spectral forms wavering between clarity and dissolution. Some appeared almost solid, their features distinct enough that I could see the confusion in their eyes.

Others were barely wisps, fading in and out of perception.

An older woman in a nightgown reached for me, her mouth moving in silent pleas.

"I'm sorry," I said, my heart constricting. "I'll come back for you, I promise."

A businessman with a gaping wound in his chest struggled against invisible bindings. I made a mental note to have Aurora teach me what that might mean, but I suspected some kind of hex. "I'll do what I can to help you, I promise."

A child, no more than seven, sat cross-legged in mid-air, playing with toys that weren't there. He didn't seem in distress, only lonely.

Each one I passed left a mark on my conscience, a silent accusation.

You cannot save everyone, my mate's voice echoed in my head. It was as if he were there with me.

"You would say I'm hopeless," I whispered to him, "but I can't just leave them here."

Ghost nuzzled my hand, her touch like the memory of warmth as she urged me to stay on task.

"I know," I said, hating myself for not being able to help the lost. "Focus. The Aldrichs are alive, and it's up to me to keep them that way. I'll speak to Death about these ghosts and make sure they get to move on to the afterlife, one way or another."

But Killion wasn't entirely wrong. I did want to save everyone, and my necromancy made my chest itch, wishing to call these souls back to the human world.

A man in torn clothing materialized directly in my

path, his face contorted in anguish. "Help me," he begged, his voice sounding like it traveled through water to reach me. "I don't belong here."

"I know," I replied, adjusting my grip on my blade. "And I swear I'll help as many of you as possible, but not right now. I need to find someone. Silas Mercer. He's a hunter in the physical realm. Have you seen him?"

The spirit's face clouded with confusion, then fear. "The chains... Stay away from the chains," he muttered before disappearing into the mist.

Spirits here sometimes spoke in riddles or fragments, their minds fractured by their incomplete transition. Even though I knew that, something about his warning ratcheted up my wariness. I swallowed, keeping a firm grip on Ghost. "That's not too ominous."

Regardless,. I squared my shoulders and continued forward, each step carrying me deeper into the domain between the living and the dead. Ghost paused, nose twitching, before bearing sharply to the left.

"Got something?" I followed. Stretching across the colorless terrain, dim yellow lines appeared in a grid.

Ley lines. The supernatural world, equivalent to power cables, casting just enough illumination to navigate by. "I feel like Dorothy following the yellow brick road," I said. "As long as there are no flying monkeys, right?"

Ghost ignored me, sniffing along one of the lines. Whispers grew louder as we progressed, a cacophony of pleas, memories, and regrets that threatened to overwhelm my senses.

Help us...

Please, I'm not supposed to be here...
Tell my daughter I'm sorry...

My tattoo burned, and my palm itched. These stuck souls needed to be reaped.

Ghost yipped, the sound distorted in the thick atmosphere. Even as my necromancy and my heart felt more and more remorseful, her hackles rose, and my scythe jerked in my hand. The blade glowed with the same light as the ley line beneath us.

The pull was undeniable, like a compass finding north. I allowed it to guide me, feeling the vibration intensify with each step. It was as if the blade was letting me know I was getting warmer.

As those vibrations grew more insistent, they became almost painful against my palm. Through the mist, a dark silhouette materialized, barely distinguishable from the surrounding gloom.

"I don't think that's a soul," I said. "Is it?"

Ghost shook her mane, but her hackles were still up. Whatever it was, it was dangerous.

As we cautiously approached, the mass seemed to expand, stretching upward and outward until it reached at least twelve feet high. That's when I heard it—the clink of chains.

The bands were heavy and circled its massive form, draped across huge shoulders and tight around limbs that ended in elongated claws.

There was another clink, a sound that shouldn't have carried in this muffled environment, but somehow penetrated directly into my bones. "Why is my blade leading us to this thing?"

Ghost growled, the fur along her spine rising even higher. She positioned herself in front of me. My scythe jerked me forward, and I careened into her, nearly sending both of us sprawling to the ground.

"Dude," I snapped at the blade, "what in the grim reaper are you doing?"

It pulsed urgently, practically singing with energy. The massive entity slowly turned in our direction. Its face —if you could call it that—was a void darker than the surrounding area. There was only the faint suggestion of hollow eye sockets and a gaping maw.

"Please tell me that's not Silas Mercer having a really bad hair day."

Whatever this thing was, my reaper weapon was convinced it was what we'd been seeking. My psychopomp's answering whine suggested she was thoroughly confused as well.

I froze, torn between my screaming instincts to run and the pull of my weapon urging me on.

The creature fully noticed us, its attention focused on something I couldn't see. That's when I spotted the threads of energy, thinner than dental floss but filled with an unnatural red light. They extended from the monster's body and disappeared into the ether.

I rubbed my thumb along the scythe's handle. "Those are connected to something in our world."

Ghost's ears flattened against her head. As we watched, the threads pulsated rhythmically. They took up a beat that I recognized—heartbeats.

"Not what I was expecting," I murmured, studying the monster. "Mercer has somehow inserted his essence into this thing to keep someone like me at bay. What do you want to bet those threads are connected to our vampire family? Smart, and also, super annoying."

I spun the blade handle in my hand, running through my options.

I couldn't kill the thing, because doing so might also kill the Aldrichs. I couldn't disconnect the threads, because that might do the same. I had hoped it might be as easy as simply walking up to Mercer and dropping that pin on him, but nothing was ever easy.

Being a vet had taught me that sometimes the scariest, most aggressive animal in the room is the one that needs the most help. Of course, animals aren't usually twelve-foot monstrosities with chains for accessories and a face like a black hole, but the same principle might still apply.

"Okay, Ghost. Time to play tag with the nightmare factory."

I dug into the bag and pulled out the bespelled push-pin. It looked ordinary, just a metal pin with a colorful plastic head, but it buzzed in my palm and bounced around erratically.

I closed my hand to keep from losing it. "Whoa, easy there, Mr. Pin. Save that energy for the tall, dark, and horrifying beast over there."

It pricked me, and I bit back a curse as I shuffled closer, wondering how good my aim was. It had been a while since I'd played darts with Nita at our favorite karaoke bar, but I had a monster-sized target to hit.

All I need to do is tag it, I reminded myself, trying to steady my breathing. "This is no different than pinning the tail on the donkey, except the donkey is a soul sucking monster, and missing it means potentially dying here. No pressure."

Ghost's lips peeled back from her teeth as the chained thing stepped forward to meet our advance. The pushpin jumped more frantically, trying to squeeze out between my fingers. Each step closer made my heart hammer against my ribs. The air grew so frigid that my lungs ached with each breath.

The chains snapped taut with a sound like a gunshot, and the creature's massive form stilled. All of its attention zeroed in on me.

I couldn't see eyes in those sockets, yet I felt its gaze all the same—a piercing, hungry awareness that sent ice down my spine. "Hey," I said casually, because my brain's default setting is awkward when terrified. "Don't mind us. Just passing through."

Each of the links in the chains was etched with symbols that moved when I focused on them. For a crazy second, I wondered what my veterinary school class-mates would say if they could see me now. Chloe Frost: graduated with honors, died trying to stick a magical pushpin into a chain monster. Not exactly the career trajectory outlined in my five-year plan.

Without warning, I felt the tether in my chest give a tug. My lungs warmed, as if Killion were breathing heat into them.

"Looks like it's now or never," I told Ghost. "We're about to get yanked back."

The air around us crackled, and the hair on my arms stood on end. I held the pushpin in one hand and the scythe in the other. I lunged and threw for center mass.

It made contact, sinking into the shadowy form as if the monster were made of butter. For a split second, nothing happened.

Then the thing roared.

The sound was more than physical—it bypassed my ears and reverberated inside my skull. Rage and pain echoed in my brain, a combination that made me want to claw at it to make it stop.

The creature convulsed, its form ripping and twisting like smoke in a whirlwind. Threads of golden light erupted from the point where the pushpin had disappeared, spreading across its body like cracks in ice.

I stumbled backward, feeling a surge of triumph.

That triumph was short-lived. Its body began to expand and widen, darkness pouring from it like water. The chains lashed out in all directions, and I threw up an arm to defend myself.

They whipped through the air with purpose, seeking a target—me.

The first one struck like a bull whip, slicing across my arm. Pain blazed white-hot, and I bit back a scream. I swung my blade in a desperate arc, trying to remember my training, but those lessons seemed so much easier when I wasn't facing a nightmare creature in the in-between.

A second chain wrapped around my thigh and yanked. I crashed to the spongy ground, my breath punching from my lungs as spectral dust billowed up around me.

I slashed at the chain and Ghost pounced at the monster, sinking her teeth into its buttery flesh. The thing howled and released me.

I whacked the metal links with my blade, and the chain recoiled. Blood trickled down my leg and arm. Each heartbeat sent fresh waves of agony through me.

Although the monster had retreated at Ghost's attack, it raged at me again. I deflected another blow. "We need to get out of here," I yelled at my psychopomp.

A link sliced across my cheek, and I tasted copper. The monster loomed larger, feeding on my fear. The energy threads pulsed with malevolent light.

Ghost pounced on me, her fur radiant like moonlight, and her eyes blazing with protective fury. The monster hesitated, faltering momentarily as she growled with otherworldly power and took my wrist between her jaws.

I tugged on the tether at the same time.

The monster struck her with a fist.

She released me with a bark of pain, but she inserted herself between us and took the hit of another swing.

"No!" I screamed, rage replacing my fear. I grabbed onto her tightly and sent a message down the channel to Killion. *"Get us out of here. Now!"*

The anchor pulled at my essence, as if I were being sucked through a cosmic straw. The in-between warped around us, its gray palette bleeding back into a kaleidoscope of colors. My stomach lurched as reality bent, stretched, and finally snapped back into place.

I gasped as the frigid chill gave way to the warmth and humidity of Shepherd's Rest once more.

The familiar silhouettes of weathered headstones

materialized from the haze. Moonlight filtered through the oak branches, casting dappled shadows across the crossroads and the ritual circle.

The transition was so abrupt that my senses couldn't handle it. One moment I was fighting for my life and the realm of the in-between, and the next—

My knees buckled beneath me. I collapsed to the ground, my blade clattering beside me. Each breath came in ragged gasps as warm blood trickled down my nose, arm, and thigh.

"Chloe!" three voices called out in unison.

I spit blood onto the ground. My ears rang like I'd survived the front row of a death metal concert. Even Ghost, morphing back to her five-pound puppy form, drooped beside me, exhausted.

Through my blurred vision, I saw. He reached for me. Aurora and Andy did too, their faces masks of worry illuminated by the dim moonlight.

"I'm fine," I tried to say, but it came out as an unconvincing groan.

Killion's hands roamed my body as his eyes scanned my injuries. "You're bleeding," he said with tight rage in every word.

"Her pupils are dilated, and she might have a broken nose." Aurora tipped my face up to study it better. "Did you get hit in the head?"

"No, but the Ghost Lands know how to throw a welcome back party. I feel like I've been hit with a sledgehammer."

Killion frowned at my wounds. "Can you stand?"

"Probably. Eventually. Maybe." I went to try, but pain

shot through my thigh, even without any weight being placed on it. "With help."

He slid an arm around my waist while Andy supported me on the other side. Together, they lifted me to my feet with surprising gentleness.

"Next time, I'm bringing a bigger scythe. Or a flamethrower. Does fire work on monsters?"

"Monsters?" Aurora said. "You mean ghosts?"

"There were plenty of those, but what attacked me was a...thing wrapped in chains. I think it's something Mercer has created and that it's attached to the Aldrichs."

"Let's focus on getting you patched up before planning your next suicide mission," Killion said, his voice so tight with emotion, I was surprised he could speak.

"A monster," Aurora repeated, retrieving my blade from the ground and sticking it in my bag. "What kind?"

I nodded, regretting the motion as the cemetery tilted sideways. "It was more of a...blob, but sentient and protective of two threads that were connected to it. They pulsed like heartbeats."

"And the pushpin?" she asked.

"I stuck it on the thing, and I think it worked. The monster absorbed it."

She found her parchment map and unrolled it. A smile lit her face. "Got him."

Killion's arm tightened around my waist, steadying me as I swayed. He and Andy moved me to a flat grave marker and eased me down on it so I could sit. "You did well. But if you ever scare me like that again, I'll—"

"Lock me in the penthouse?"

"At the very least," he replied.

The pain was spreading, hot and insistent, and I grimaced. "I need to check on Ghost."

"Andy will check on her. You stay still."

He placed one hand on my thigh and the other on my arm as Andy moved to my dog's side. Warmth spread from Killion's touch, a tingling sensation that reminded me of my body responding to a shot of caffeine. The pain began to recede, replaced by a pleasant numbness, as his vampire magic stopped the bleeding and encouraged the wounds to heal.

I closed my eyes, enjoying the magic flowing through me. "I think the threads were feeding lines," I told them. "As we suspected, Mercer's using Cormac and Rome to elevate his power."

My skin began to knit itself back together, and even though I could still feel phantom pain where the chains had struck, it was tolerable. Killion worked on my nose next.

Aurora turned the map for us to see, murmuring something in Gaelic. The paper responded, rippling as though caught in an invisible breeze. A small dot of light appeared, blinking steadily near the edge of town. "That's the old Backwater brewery," she said. "It was known for its tunnels where they stored the beer vats. Abandoned since the 90s when a batch of toxic beer killed a group of frat boys."

"Yikes," I muttered, standing up with only a slight wobble. I wiggled my now fixed nose and wiped away the last of the blood. "I don't suppose their ghosts are still hanging around? Nothing says 'perfect hostage holding area' like a building with its own set of spirits who died tragically."

Killion stood beside me, his hand supporting my elbow. "Isolated, surrounded by empty lots, with multiple access points through the brewing tunnels...it is a good place to hide."

"And excellent acoustics for screaming," Andy added grimly as he carried Ghost to us.

She blinked at me with sleepy eyes, but her wound was already gone.

I scratched behind her ears. "Okay, then. How do we get to this abandoned brewery of doom?"

11

The abandoned brewery parking lot was overgrown with weeds. Part of the roof had caved in, and the real estate sign was barely visible near the street, having tipped over at some point and faded in the hot southern sun.

"On this week's episode of Real Estate for the Dead, we explore the ruins of a one-time state-of-the-art brewery," Andy said in an announcer voice as we approached. "The building, currently unoccupied and selling to the right buyer for the low price of totally free, once turned out over ten thousand bottles of premium beer a month. Now, the only thing it's turning out is a sense of menace. Call 1-800-Underworld for your showing. But hurry—properties like this in our Haunted Lives of the Dead and Not-So-Famous are going fast!"

"It has potential." I stepped over the carcass of a raccoon. As always, my inner grim reached for the animal's soul, and I had to suffocate the urge to bring it back to life.

Neither Killion nor Aurora laughed. We made our way past the boarded-up double doors and a second metal doorway where most of the corrugated sheet metal hung in rusting tatters.

The interior didn't look much better. Dusty and broken beer bottles lay scattered across the floor. The smell of mold and stale hops lingered in the back of my throat.

I scanned the vast, hollow space. Not only had it seen better days, but they were now blurry, hungover memories. The ceiling soared at least twenty feet above us, giving it the feel of an aircraft hangar or a less welcoming version of one of those weird warehouse-sized hipster bars. Graffiti plastered every surface, and I admired the work of someone called Streaks who took the time to spray paint their name across the wall no fewer than ten times.

Killion slipped his hand into mine. "Our primary focus is to locate the Aldrichs, but we know that Silas Mercer has been dealing in black magic. Watch out for traps and keep your shields up."

Ghost trotted at my heels. A few souls lingered in the rafters. They were as tattered and miserable-looking as the brewery itself. "Our list of souls to send to the afterlife is growing," I told the dog.

As we made our way deeper inside, Aurora and Andy following a short distance behind us, I saw a band of old bikers who wore leather and seemed angry about having met the business end of their life contracts. I had slipped my scythe's leather holder onto my back when we'd left the limo and now drew the blade from it. They flickered from existence.

Killion's phone rang, and he stopped to answer it. "Katarina, we are at the Backwater Brewery."

I slipped away with Ghost to examine a seating area where folks had once gathered to enjoy each other's company. In an instant, the biker gang rematerialized in a threatening semicircle around me. At least, it would've been threatening if they hadn't all been a little on the see-through side.

"What do you want?" one of them growled, his bushy mustache quivering like a squirrel's tail. From his stance and prominent belly, I suspected he might be the leader.

"I'm searching for a still-living human who is dabbling in black magic. But as long as we're going to have this conversation, I can help you."

I flashed my blade at him.

"Help?" another said. He had a cloudy beard and was missing an eye. "Or finish us off?"

Ghost bared her teeth with a cute little snarl, and they seemed amused. Only for a fraction of a second, though. When she morphed into her psychopomp form, all of them floated a significant step back.

I toyed with the blade and stroked her fur. "There's only one way this is going down. I cross you over, and it's all puppies and sunshine. Your other choice is to stay and rot like this place."

"We like it here," Beer Belly said. "We ain't going nowhere."

Killion joined me, and he was able to see this group of spirits. "We don't have time for this," he said.

The gang sized him up, and the leader snarled. "You don't belong here."

I tapped the blade against my leg. "You're the ones who don't belong here. It's time for you to go."

A flick of the man's wrist, and one of his subordinates charged me with a roar. He went right through me, and the experience was less than comfortable. A chilly sensation prickled my limbs, and my tattoo flared to life. When he made a second pass, all I had to do was shift the blade to catch him in his middle, and he froze.

Ghost chomped down on his arm and disappeared with him, hauling him to the afterlife before he could blink.

The rest of the gang decided not to stick around. It's amazing how brave they are when they think they have the upper hand, and how fast that disappears when their leader rides his heavenly Harley off into the afterlife.

Before they could disappear, I spun in a circle and released my scythe like a Frisbee, cutting the rest of them loose from their worldly tethers. Ghost wasn't back yet, but they moved on anyway.

Killion grabbed me by the hand and tugged me with him, snatching up the scythe and giving it back to me. "Harlow and Katarina will be here in a few minutes with some backup."

Sweat slid down the back of my shoulders, and a new ghost flickered in and out like a shorted-out neon sign. This one wasn't part of the gang, and if I had to guess, I'd say he might be one of the frat boys who had died from the bad beer.

Honestly, I hadn't realized it was a thing.

Some of the hiding shadows materialized as more spirits, drawn by my weapon. Some of them Killion could see, others he couldn't.

Most of the time, those who were stuck in this dimension ran from me, but some of them wanted to cross over and didn't know how. That seemed to be the case with this group. Their sheer number made my skin crawl as they crowded around us. There were too many to reap individually, too many even to count, and they all began to shout over each other in a confused mess of voices.

I flinched and was grateful when Ghost reappeared. "I have to cross them," I said to Killion. "I know it's not part of our agenda, but I can't just leave them here." I wasn't even sure I could get past all of them. The amount of frantic energy was compounding, and their ability to become more stable and physical.

"Do what you must do." He called over his shoulder to our companions. "Let's split up. Chloe and I will take the tunnel that's directly ahead. The two of you scout for the other. If you find any sign of Mercer, send a text and we'll join you."

Andy snapped off a salute. "Is it bad?"

I nodded. "Lots of stuck souls here."

"I wonder why?" Aurora said. "No mass casualties have been reported in this place. Could it be that Mercer's dark magic is drawing lost souls here?"

That was as good a guess as any. "All I know is that I'm going to have to send most of them to their happy place, or I'm not going to be able to locate our kidnapper anytime soon."

It took Ghost and me close to ten minutes to clear a

path through the lingering spirits. Some were angry, others were lost, and others were fearful. All in all, though, they all wanted to escape this place.

As Killion and I continued forward, I wiped my blade on my pants. "This place is full of weird vibes." We passed a bottling machine. "I can only give it two stars on Yelp."

My humor was pointless. The master vampire didn't even crack a smile.

Both mine and Killion's phones buzzed with a group text from Aurora. *Found this schematic of the building.*

Killion skimmed it and responded. *Let's meet at the bar if we haven't found Mercer in twenty.*

We turned the corner and pulled up short. Another group of ghosts huddled together, blocking the hallway. Some panicked, others seemed oblivious. A few were more transparent than others, suggesting they had been there for a longer period.

"Reapers creepers," I mumbled. "What is going on here?" I tightened my grip on my scythe. "Soul Management Group needs to give me a raise."

Killion was nearly beside himself. "We don't have time for this."

"You said that already." I understood where he was coming from, but I had no choice in the matter. "This is what happens when you're married to a grim."

Typically, I strived to make the transition to the afterlife as easy and stress-free as possible for the spirit, but tonight, I had to put efficiency ahead of my empathy. I hefted the blade and winged it again, slicing the group in half. Ghost ran and collected all of them in a mighty leap.

The path was now clear, and we continued. I couldn't help but stew over all the souls stuck here, as well as those still lingering in the in-between. My cuts were gone, my nose normal, and the bruises had vanished, but I was left with an uncomfortable sensation in my chest. My heart ached for all of them, regardless of what they'd done or how they'd ended up stuck and lingering where they weren't supposed to be.

Killion's expression was careful and calculating as he studied the map on his phone, guiding us to the main tunnel. When Ghost reappeared, she was a puppy again and bolted off into the dark ahead of us.

I called after her, worried she might run into Mercer or some monster he had created. She might even run into more spirits.

"She'll be fine," Killion assured me. "It is you I worry about. You have exerted an enormous amount of energy tonight. How do you feel?"

"Outside of starving and being frustrated because I couldn't take care of the spirits in the in-between, I'm doing okay. I'm concerned about what we'll find if we do locate Mercer, though."

"You sent several dozen ghosts to the afterlife. You freed them from this world. That's a good thing. You can work it out with Death about those stuck in the in-between. For now, let me worry about Mercer. When we find him, you must allow me to interrogate him."

"I know, I know. Now that we're close, can you pick up anything about him or the Aldrichs?"

His nostrils flared as he scented the air. He closed his eyes, and I felt him sending out his magic like sonar to see if he could pick up on any vampires in the area. When he opened his eyes again, he shook his head. "I don't believe they're here."

That realization made my heart sink. "When we catch Mercer, we'll get the truth out of him. We'll find out where he's hiding them."

"You're not failing anyone, you know," Killion said. He must have read my mind. "Not my nest and not the ghosts. Your empathy makes you unique, but your over-achieving, perfectionist personality is taking a toll on you. Clear your mind and focus. You must be at the top of your game when we encounter him."

Overachieving perfectionist? That summed it up, but it made me feel worse that he had to point it out.

Rebar tangled overhead like a metal spider's web. Mold crept in fuzzy patches across the ceiling and floor of the tunnel. There was nothing homey about a factory. Nothing comforting. But even the stale, haunted main floor was better than the overwhelming, ominous dark-ness of the tunnel.

I couldn't help it—I ordered Ghost to return to us. Her nails echoed down the narrow passageway as we avoided crumbling bits of wall and patches of debris.

Even if Mercer wasn't here at the moment, I expected to find traces of him. Food. Gear. Any kind of sign that he had been here. And where was his dog?

"You don't think this is a trap, do you?" I asked. We turned into another branch of the tunnel, and I felt a new layer of dread as it sloped downward.

"That is a possibility."

He didn't seem daunted by the idea. I didn't want to

admit how much I hated this. How much I wanted to be back above ground, and where I could see more than a few feet in front of me.

We passed several metal vats and a storage area that had been vandalized long ago. Ghost appeared, and I scooped her into my arms, nuzzling her neck. She was warm. Goosebumps covered my skin like they did when I walked through the freezer aisle at the grocery store. I prayed no more spirits were hanging around, causing the drop in temperature.

She squirmed, her body vibrating with excitement. A cold, hard cement wall stood before us at the end of the tunnel. My heart sank again. "Is that a dead end? It wasn't on the map, was it?"

Killion looked like he might say something, then glanced at me and back to the wall, scrutinizing it.

A further drop in temperature. The frosty air hollowed out my throat and tickled my nose. My gravesite slipped into place instinctively, and I saw the edges of the wall glowing.

"The wall is an illusion," I told Killion. "What do you want to bet he's on the other side?"

The master vampire tunneled into his magic and energy burst from him, slamming into the illusionary wall. My own magic responded, sending a second wave at it. The wall fell away.

On the other side, an unfinished, uninviting room appeared.

Ghost yelped and wiggled so hard that I couldn't control her. She launched from my arms and hit the ground running, scrambling inside.

I jetted after her, wondering if Mercer and possibly the Aldrichs would be waiting.

Ghost yelped again, louder, and I pivoted in a circle, searching for Mercer, but not seeing him. A swirling mist moved in the corner of my eye, and magic crackled against my nerves.

"Silas Mercer," I said, feeling Killion slip into the room with me. "Show yourself."

The place was full of power and potential, and I had the overwhelming sensation that the mist was about to attack. Instead, it slipped past me.

I yanked my scythe from its holder and sliced through it.

Silas Mercer, standing only a few feet away with his hat pulled low and his hands in the pockets of his duster, appeared like he didn't have a care in the world. He gave me an evil smile.

I'd cut through his illusion. He was no phantom image, and this was no trap.

When I smiled back, the grin faded from his face. It was replaced by shock. He'd believed I wouldn't be able to see him. Now, he grappled with how his invisibility had failed.

I pointed the blade at his heart. "Welcome to my world, Mercer. Start talking."

12

The world seemed too slow, taking a lifetime between each beat of my heart. Everything was muted, like it had switched to silent mode and was running in the background.

"He's here?" Killion asked, his voice sounding distant, even though he was only a few feet from me.

I didn't take my focus off Mercer. "You can't see him?"

The master vampire looked vexed as he followed my pinpoint gaze. "All I see is a swirling fog."

Ghost barked, the sound as soft as cotton. She sniffed the ground in a circle, as if trying to pick up Mercer's trail.

Why couldn't they see him?

Why could I?

Because I can walk between worlds.

The eerie realization that I had crossed into another dimension skipped through my mind. I wasn't completely in it because I could still see my companions and our target, but I was not entirely in their world either. A different type of in-between.

I didn't want to take my eyes off Mercer, but I couldn't help it. I scanned in both directions, triple-checking that I wasn't in the Ghost Lands. Mercer observed me, and I couldn't confirm that he was solid. He appeared to be, but looks could be deceiving.

I wiggled my blade at him. "Where are the Aldrichs?"

The smirk he gave me made my blood boil. He knew I was grappling with the fact that I was the only one who could see his true form. He liked that I was disoriented.

Then everything went silent, including my pulse. The silence filled every part of me. My tattoo burned hot. I inhaled sharply, and the bitter silence filled my lungs.

The scythe whispered, "*Kill.*"

Then it moved on its own accord, swinging through the air.

Mercer moved faster than I could have anticipated, and the blade only caught the edge of his bicep.

He cried out.

I exhaled, and everything snapped back into place. The world stopped being muted. Killion surged forward, now able to see him, and grabbed him by his lapels, slamming him against the stone tunnel wall.

Ghost morphed into psychopomp form and bared her teeth at the man.

"Gotcha," I said, my entire body trembling. I felt faint.

But all of the thoughts crowding into my brain disappeared as fast as they came.

Killion pounded Mercer against the stones. "Tell me where you are keeping them."

"Not here," he snapped. "You found me, but only me."

The scythe vibrated, the longing to strike him again

evident. I kept a tight clamp on it. "This ends now. You're out of choices." *You're out of time.*

Mercer's eyes grew dark with a violent, angry maelstrom. The smirk disappeared, replaced with a dead serious expression of a man who realized this was his last stand. "As long as I have them, I always have a choice."

Killion snarled. Ghost echoed it.

My mind reeled. Mercer was right. We could threaten and torture him, but he still might be able to keep the vampire family hidden from us.

I had to approach this in a different way. Going head to head with this monster wasn't going to work. The harder we pushed, the harder he would dig in his heels.

"You might say they're on life support," he smirked.

Killion's arm slammed against his throat. "What does that mean?"

Mercer coughed, closing his eyes and gritting his teeth. He pushed at Killion, but he could not move the master vampire, no matter what dark magic he'd been working.

"I have orders to reap you," I told him. It was the only thing I could think to use as a bargaining tool. "Tell us where they are, and I will work out a deal with Soul Management Group to extend your contract."

Killion whirled his head. "What?"

Mercer made choking noises, desperate to free himself from my mate's hold. "I'm already...dead. Your precious group found me and forced me...into this life long ago."

I frowned. Killion released him. The blade trembled, and it was everything I could do to keep it at my side, its blood lust all-consuming as it tried over and over to get to him. "What are you talking about?"

Slowly, he straightened, rubbing at his neck and shooting daggers at Killion. His voice came out rough because of his damaged vocal cords. "You heard me. SMG forced me into this life."

My anger retreated. Disbelief took its place. "You're lying."

He raised dirty fingers. "Two things you need to know, little girl. First,"—he waggled one digit—"your precious vampires are tied to me. If you kill me, they die. And second,"—another waggle—"SMG is hiding more secrets than you can count. I'm one of them."

I took a step back. The blade fought me, and I had to put my other hand on it to keep it from leaping from my grip and harvesting his soul. "So you're saying that if I reap you—"

Mercer watched me, his eyes sharp like a hawk's. "They'll die," he finished. "Slowly and painfully."

Killion swore in several languages. I mentally did the same. I wanted to dismiss it as a ploy to keep us off balance, but I saw the hopelessness and despair behind the rage in Mercer's eyes.

I thought back to the chains around the monster. "Why would they force you into servitude?"

"You haven't earned the right to that story yet, little girl."

I wanted to reap him just for calling me that. "I'm not a little girl. That's condescending, so knock it off. You've made your point about the vampire family. I'm willing to hear you out. But there's only so much I will tolerate, so if you want to work out a deal, I suggest you start convincing me why I shouldn't simply torture the information out of you before I follow through with my orders."

He straightened to his full height, glancing between me and Killion. Andy, Aurora, Katarina, and Harlow rushed down the tunnel, catching up with us and forming a wall at my back. Ghost eased closer to Mercer, still showing her teeth.

"Where are the Aldrichs?" Harlow demanded.

"Not here," Killion said with an undercurrent of fury.

The hunter was smart enough to realize he wasn't getting out of this unscathed. His attention refocused on me. "I'll tell you what you want to know in exchange for your promise to help me."

My heart grasped at the straw. I needed something, anything, to save that family. "I can't promise anything until you tell me what you want. I'm willing to do what I can, though, and that's the best deal you're going to get."

"I want justice for my family. Give me that, and I'll tell you everything."

"What happened to them?"

"SMG promised to help me find the rogue vampire nest responsible for my family's death. It was brutal. Horrible. Slow and painful." The words echoed those he'd used before. "Instead, they cursed me to become an unwilling hunter, systematically destroying supernatural communities they considered liabilities."

Liabilities? The curse. The chains.

None of us moved. We didn't even breathe.

"That's not possible," I said. "SMG only deals with

souls. They have no say over who lives or dies unless their soul contract is up."

He gave a dry laugh. "Don't be stupid. They have far more power than that. At least, a few of them do. They hide behind the front that they show you reapers. They keep you in the dark, meek and gullible, forcing you to do their bidding. Behind the curtain, they make decisions about life and death that would curl your toes. Anyone who catches on or threatens to expose them suddenly finds their life contract has expired. Like me."

Was it a coincidence that Death had given me the assignment to reap Mercer right after he'd kidnapped the Aldrichs, bringing him to our attention?

Killion telepathically said, *You can't possibly believe him.*

Truth was, I did. Not entirely, but things didn't add up. "I need proof."

"I'll get it for you. The curse ties me to all those I've killed. Death will not sever those ties. My afterlife will be nothing but torment, and the souls connected to me will be lost in that torment forever. You find a way to break the curse, and I'll reveal the location of the vampire family."

Before I could respond, the mastiff appeared from out of thin air. Mercer grabbed its scruff, and the two of them vanished.

13

On Monday morning, the reception desk at Frosty Paws looked like a paper castle, an untidy fortress of Post-it note ramparts and appointment list tourists.

I was the exhausted queen, presiding over it all. My faithful knight, Sylvie, had come in early for a quick orientation and was already on the job, answering phone calls that kept pouring in. Patients were reporting a mysterious rash and other ailments in a variety of pets, from canines to reptiles.

I tried calling her Vi, but it didn't seem to match her personality or enthusiasm. "I think Sylvie is better," I told her. "It's more you."

She winked. "That's what my father always said, too. Maybe you're right."

I obsessively checked my phone for Death's response to my request to speak to him about Silas Mercer. So far, he'd been AWOL, and I had the nagging sense it was because he was hiding the truth from me.

Killion and the others were searching the area surrounding the brewery. He'd devised a grid and assigned each of his team a section to hunt for the Aldrichs. We all suspected they were still invisible because of Mercer's magic, but after our encounter with the hunter, Killion blamed himself for not forcing Mercer to give up their location.

"Is it always like this on Mondays?" Sylvia asked.

I stuck my phone in my back pocket, catching a tower of files before they fell off the corner of the desk. "Yes and no."

The waiting room was filling up with wagging tails and shifting human impatience, the way it had on April Fools'. "I had to close early on Saturday, so some of these folks are rollovers, but Mondays tend to be a bit messy. Pets are like kids—they tend to get sick at night or on the days when the clinic is closed."

She balanced the handset between her ear and shoulder while fanning herself with one of the lists she'd written. "We have air-conditioning, right?"

It was supposed to get into the 80s again today. "I'll check the thermostat, but yes, we do. Unfortunately, it's as old as this building and doesn't always work well. Another thing to add to my to-do list—call the heating and air guy and have him give it a check-up."

"Is the number in our contacts?" At my nod, she waved me off. "I'll handle it."

The door chime alerted us to more arrivals, and two more clients trailed in. A slobbering Labrador trotted in with an older couple who wore matching glasses, and a nervous-looking kid towed a bunny nearly as big as himself. Sylvie switched calls while also placating a Chihuahua with a box of treats, as she spoke into the receiver. "Yes, of course, Mrs. Daily. Dr. Chloe is the best, and she will be happy to see Astro this afternoon at two forty-five."

Her fingers flew over the keyboard. She replaced the handset and beamed at the boy with the rabbit as I hurried down the hall to check the thermostat. It was set correctly, but I had the feeling it would struggle to keep up today.

Now, if I could get ahead of the appointments rolling in. Where was JR?

I fired off a text asking if everything was okay before I marched back to grab my first patient. While I appreciated all of my skills, whether they came from being a reaper, my vampire turning, or the tiny bit of dragon magic I'd picked up from Killion, the fact was, none of that was going to help this new veterinarian handle her booming business.

A heavy-set woman with shocking pink lipstick brushed forward to corner me before I could grab my patient's chart. She talked animatedly about her three cats—Chip, Cookie, and Pudding—going into lengthy detail about their various likes, dislikes, and hygiene habits. I kept trying to interrupt her, but I discovered that she and her felines were my first patients.

"Why don't you bring them back?" I said, taking one of their carriers.

She grabbed the other two and followed. "Chip only likes pâté," she told me as she set his carrier on the exam table. "Cookie has to eat only crunchy food or she gets sick."

We opened up the carriers, and all three cats reared back.

"Pudding is the cranky one, right?" I asked with a polite smile.

In the back of my mind, I was still thinking about Mercer. Would SMG officially kick me out if I didn't reap him? I wasn't convinced he was telling the truth, but I suspected he had some skills that I could utilize if I could recruit him to help me investigate those inside the organization that I suspected had none of our best interests at heart.

"That's right!" She nodded enthusiastically. "You must have read their file. A rare thing these days. The last vet I went to made me tell him their history every time we went for an appointment. So frustrating!"

I hadn't read the file, but she'd provided a litany of information that had penetrated my other thoughts. Plus, my reaper skills came with a side of ESP. I'd always had the ability to sense what was wrong with an animal long before any test or scans confirmed it. "We want your experience with us to always be a positive one," I told her.

All three cats were relatively healthy, and I was able to administer the necessary immunizations and send them on their way within a few minutes. At the front desk, I perked up when Mason carried in a tray of drinks from The Smoking Bean. "Thought you might need a pick me up," the kid said.

I reached for the iced latte while he offered Sylvie her choice of coffees. "Why aren't you in school?" I asked.

"I have a free period first thing on Mondays," he said. "Mom told me you didn't get much sleep over the weekend. I figured you needed your fix."

Harlow was amazing. Boy, did I owe her. "Thank you. If you see your mom before I do, tell her I appreciate it."

I introduced Sylvie, and she leaned across the desk to fist bump him. "I already feel spoiled on my first day."

He grinned. "Come by the Bean anytime I'm working, and I'll be sure you get a discount."

"Oh, you work there?" The phone buzzed, and she reached for it.

"I'm saving for college," he told her.

She gave him a thumbs-up as she answered the phone.

He glanced around the waiting room. "Sorry, I can't stay and help, but I have a physics test at ten. I'd better go over my notes one more time."

I shooed him toward the exit. "Good luck with it."

As he left, I double-checked my phone, hoping Death or JR had responded. There were no messages or calls.

I grabbed the top file on the stack and quickly reviewed the name. "Ms. Duchamp?"

A young woman with a kitten not much bigger than Sylvie's came forward.

"Thank you for calling Frosty Paws." Sylvie's sunny voice chased us to the back.

I was upfront again an hour later, handing Tyler Lawson a cream for his rabbit's rash. It had unusual borders and didn't fit the profile of anything I'd seen before. JR had arrived and said it was probably nothing more than a common skin irritation caused by the rabbit's new bedding. I'd taken a sample of skin cells and would analyze them as soon as I had a break. "Apply this twice a day for now. If it gets worse, come back for a follow-up, okay?"

The boy nodded and left. Apparently, he had a free period this morning as well.

An Irish setter staggered through the clinic door, soggy, red-eyed, and looking suspiciously hung over. As he and his owner crossed the linoleum, a puddle spread on the tile beneath them, accompanied by tufts of the setter's fur. When his owner stopped him in order to pocket a set of car keys, the dog trailed its wet tail across the legs of an already anxious terrier, sending the smaller canine into a fit of frenzied barking that set off another round of yapping across the entire waiting room.

Sylvia wrinkled her nose. "What's going on with this guy?" she muttered.

I studied the dog across the distance. "Looks like he ran away from home and got himself in trouble."

The pair made it to the desk, and my immediate thought was of possible poisoning. I was already mentally shuffling my appointments to get this dog to the exam room as soon as possible.

"I don't know what happened," the owner said. His energy was panicked. "I swear he was fine Friday after we left here."

"You were here?" I asked.

He nodded. "For his yearly exam. I'm David Beech-wood, and this is Markem. Dr. O'Leary gave him a clean bill of health."

Sylvie brought up the dog's digital records and

scanned them. "Says he received his rabies immunization, and the doctor recommended Mr. Beechwood cut back on his treats. Other than that, everything was normal."

"Did anything unusual happen between then and now?" I asked. "Did he eat anything he shouldn't have? Get bit by another animal?"

"No, nothing."

I frowned. "I'm going to take Markem to the back," I told Sylvie.

"We did get caught in some rain last night on our walk," Mr. Beechwood said, pointing to the dog's neck, where it was losing the most fur. "And I bathed him several times, trying to stop the rash from spreading, but it's only gotten worse. Could he be allergic to water?"

The setter shook himself as if in response, damp drops flying everywhere. The closest patients cringed away. Sylvie glanced at me. "Seems urgent."

I reached for the dog's leash. "Come on, Markem. Let's have a look at you."

The next waiting patient balked, and Sylvie rose from behind the desk, pulling out a treat from her skirt pocket and handing it to the disgruntled man's terrier. "We'll make sure to throw in a free bag of these treats to show our appreciation for your patience."

I dodged as Markem let loose another shower of damp hair while I hustled him to the only empty exam room. The dog was patient as I donned gloves and gave him a brief once-over to check his heart, ears, and eyes.

The owner fiddled with the leash. "Could it be the rabies shot?"

I crouched beside Markem, listening to his pulse with my stethoscope, even though I had already done so. This time, however, I allowed my otherworldly senses to scan him. "Highly doubtful."

While his heart thumped with a normal *lub-dub* rhythm, the rash shimmered and pulsed with a faint luminosity I'd only seen with spirits and trapped souls.

The pulsing kept time with each beat of the setter's heart. "This is more than an ordinary allergic reaction." I thought back to the rabbit and the unusual rash it had presented with. I hadn't noticed any supernatural glow, but maybe I would when I examined the skin scrapings I'd collected. "I'd like to take a skin sample to analyze."

"Is it serious?" Mr. Beecham asked.

I had no idea. "Have you changed his bedding, food, or anything related to cleaning products or shampoo that he might've come in contact with?"

Everything I suggested, the man shook his head at. I checked the dog for fleas or other parasites; none were visible. Beyond the fact that it was no ordinary rash, I couldn't make a diagnosis or reassure the owner that it was an easy fix. "I'd like you to leave him here so I can run tests." I gave him a reassuring smile. "I'll figure this out, and I'll call you as soon as I have a full report."

He looked skeptical and a little disappointed, but just nodded. "I guess I have no choice."

He said a worried goodbye to the dog and left. I went to work gathering skin samples and labeling them before I led Markem to a kennel in the back.

His expression was as mopey as his owner's, but he seemed a bit relieved, too. Ghost trotted over to the kennel and put her nose up to it. As my psychopomp, she was immune to diseases and illnesses, but I wasn't taking any chances. "Stay back, girl," I commanded. "Until we know what's wrong with Markem, we can't be too careful."

I gave the dog a soft blanket, a bowl of food, and some water. "You'll be your old self soon."

JR and I passed each other in the hall. "I've got another unusual skin rash," I told him. "I need to look at some samples and get them analyzed."

He checked his watch and blew out his cheeks with a sigh. "Do you think the heat has something to do with it?"

All options were on the table at the moment. "Doesn't seem likely, does it?"

"Well, maybe this weird heatwave at least explains the increase in patients. I'm three behind already."

I didn't mention he was late. "Full moon isn't for another week," I said, grinning. "Gotta chalk it up to something. Might as well be the heat."

"Killion's right, you know. We need to expand. A second clinic. Or a mobile unit."

Both of which were my ideas, but I didn't correct him. "Let's get through this morning first."

We worked through lunchtime, and by three, the patient load had died down.

The cases with the mysterious rash, however, had tripled.

I called a meeting with JR, and Dr. O'Leary joined us via video. "I've analyzed the skin samples of six animals—three dogs, two cats, and a rabbit," I told them. "All show the exact same signs and symptoms, but the parasite I found in the scrapings is not one I've ever seen."

Telling them that it was a supernatural parasite would get me nowhere and wouldn't help the animals. I needed to find a real-world solution, even if the cause was magical. At least, that's where I had to start. Once I had time, I would recruit Aurora and Andy to help me determine if there was a supernatural solution.

For the next few minutes, we ran through all the possible ideas to treat the rash, dividing the patients to test different medication cocktails and see if any of them would prevent the spread. Once we could get it under control, we could then approach a treatment to heal it.

After the meeting ended, I rechecked my phone. I needed to discuss this with Death, as well as the Silas Mercer issue.

Radio silence. I was so angry and overwhelmed that I nearly threw my phone against the wall.

In order to calm myself, I marched out the back door to get a breath of fresh air.

Imagine my surprise when I discovered Death and Sylvie, heads bowed, murmuring to each other as if they were sharing secrets.

14

They huddled behind the clinic like two high schoolers sneaking a cigarette, but it wasn't nicotine they were ingesting.

Death made sweeping hand gestures, and Sylvie's head bobbed in either agreement or understanding. How was it possible she could see him? What could they possibly have to talk about?

Worse, in the next moment, they shared a laugh. I cleared my throat and slammed the door behind me with enough force that it echoed across the small expanse of lawn and tiny parking lot.

"There you are," Sylvie said in her too-cheerful voice, although it was laced with guilt. "Did you figure out what was wrong with those animals?"

"What's going on?" I asked, ignoring her.

Death shot me a fake grin that was all teeth. "This is not what it looks like."

I folded my arms and glared. "What is it then?" My eyes darted between them. "You two know each other?"

He feigned surprise. "Who, me and...Sally?"

"Sylvie," she corrected, her smile faltering for a moment. "That's my cue to leave and get back to the phones." She brushed past me. I wanted to block her way, but she was right. I could hear them ringing from back here, and I knew we had several afternoon appointments scheduled.

Most importantly, I needed to talk to my boss. "Where have you been? Why haven't you answered my messages?"

"Why haven't you reaped Silas Mercer?"

"How is it that you know Sylvie?"

He stared at me with his frosty green eyes like I was an obstinate puppy in need of obedience training. "We'll discuss her later. Right now, answer my question."

"If you'd bothered to get back to me, you'd know." I explained that we had located Mercer and discovered that he had connected himself to the Aldrichs in a way that if I reaped him, it would kill them.

"What's the problem?"

I made a disgusted noise. "They are innocent. They don't deserve to die."

"They're vampires. Their soul contracts are forfeit."

"They have a human daughter. She's missing too, remember? And regardless of your personal distaste for vampires, they didn't ask for this. They aren't rogues. They're law-abiding members of Killion's nest."

He leaned against the hood of my car, managing to look both imposing and completely at ease. A handsome, obstinate rock star who didn't need music to own his stage. "If you were called in for a performance review right now, you'd be fired."

I matched his stare, refusing to be the first to blink. "Is that what this is? A performance review?"

"Not my job." His gaze shot over my shoulder toward the door where Sylvie had disappeared.

I swiveled to look through the screen, hearing her voice in the distance as she greeted a patient. "Who is she? Did you send her?"

"Focus, Chloe. Mercer is overdue, and you have one job. Reap him. Smudgy is growing impatient."

"Maybe because they're up to something. Doesn't it seem like a big coincidence that his contract expires right when he claims he's been cursed and forced to hunt supernaturals?"

Death's expression turned flat. "Smudgy doesn't deal with hunters. We have reapers. You. Except, oh wait..." He snapped his fingers. "You're refusing to do your job. Again."

"You're acting like SMG is incapable of wrongdoing. You and I both know they aren't. You've been searching for whoever is trying to create souls out of nothing for months, and it has to be someone on the inside."

He gave me a look suggesting I was the most naïve employee he'd ever dealt with. "Mercer's claims are false. We have never hired anyone to take out supernaturals outside of the ones who dodge their termination papers. That's a bedtime story to scare rogues and noncompliant souls who try to get out of their contracts. Mercer is buying time with this ridiculous story."

"You're not even considering the idea that he might be

telling the truth. This is worth looking into. When I was in the in-between, I saw the chains on him. He *has* been cursed."

"You and your conspiracy theories. Look,"—he pushed off the hood, coming to his full height, and crossing his arms—"Mercer is out of time. His case takes precedence. Stop playing vet and get your death blade out. If you don't take care of this, you're going to find yourself on probation. Or worse. Your grim card may get cancelled. Permanently."

"Like I haven't heard that before." I restrained myself from rolling my eyes, but a seed of fear took root in my stomach. SMG could cause my permanent death, which would also cause Killion's. "Why are you being so stubborn about this?"

He stood there like an ancient statue, immovable and infuriatingly sure of his place in the world. "The universal rules will only bend so far. The vampires are not a priority, and this isn't a joke."

"So you've said. Indefinite suspension coming up." I whirled a finger like it was no big deal. His jaw tightened, and I rushed on before he could say anything. "I can stop the curse. I have to try. I'm not leaving that little girl an orphan because you're too stubborn to see what's happening and help me fix it."

For a moment, I saw doubt flicker behind his eyes. It was gone in an instant, and he stalked toward me, larger than life and as intimidating as an apocalypse. He pointed a finger at my face, and the timbre in his voice made my bones tremble. "Some things are beyond even you. You cannot fix everything. You've been given an assignment and told it is a priority. You can't keep putting your grim work on the back burner. SMG could have yanked you to headquarters ages ago and stripped you of all your power, but they didn't because you're an asset. At least you are when you *do your job*. Even now, they sent someone to help you with the clinic so that you could reprioritize and focus on the reaping. But do you? No. You go by your own agenda."

Aha. The puzzle pieces slid into place. "That's why she's so perfect. SMG sent Sylvie. Not just to help me, but to report on my activities."

"She's part of the new Internal Affairs Department I mentioned previously." He was once again expressionless, but his anger was apparent. "Do you know why we now have an IA Department? Because of you. Because you're going off on your own and doing whatever you want instead of what you've been assigned to do."

"You had renegade reapers before I came along. Remember Jacqueline?"

He snorted. "Reap the hunter and get your report to me in the next twenty-four hours. If you don't, I'm washing my hands of you." He walked a few feet away and then came to a stop. "When this ends badly—and it will—remember this conversation."

He vanished before I could ask him about the supernatural parasites. I growled in frustration.

Sylvie was organizing supplies in our tiny sales area, the picture of innocence and dedication. My hands trembled, wanting to shake her from her cheery disposition.

"Oh, hi," she said, with that annoying smile. "Need something?"

I pulled her behind the desk and lowered my voice. "You mean besides an office manager who isn't spying on me?"

She shifted on her feet, shoving her hands in her dress pockets. "My job entails keeping my true identity a secret. But I really do want to help. I admire your determination to be more than a reaper."

"Spare me," I said. "Nothing you say at this point will salvage my trust."

She sighed and dropped into the office chair. "I'm sorry. Honestly, I didn't think I would like you as much as I do. I enjoy working here, especially with you and the animals. Dr. Banks is excellent. It's only my first day, and I already feel like I've been here forever. Like this is... home."

"That was Oscar-worthy, but I'm not buying it. You're done. Head back to SMG and tell Mei that you failed your assignment."

"You're firing me?"

"Why shouldn't I?"

She came out of the chair. "I've done a great job so far, and you don't have anyone else. As busy as you are, do you think that's a good idea?"

I bit the inside of my lip. She had me there. "If you were in my position, what would you do?"

"I would put the welfare of the animals above my personal feelings. I would put professionalism for my fellow veterinarians above my personal feelings. Stressing them out doesn't help anybody."

Oh, she was good. "Guilting me into keeping you?"

Her voice held a sincere mix of desperation and

conviction. "Is there any way I can convince you to keep me on, at least for a few more days? Let me finish my probationary period and prove that I'm an awesome office manager and that my job for SMG will not interfere with that."

"Let me make this clear: betrayal is unforgivable in my book."

"So you don't have any secrets that you haven't shared with me?"

She was fighting back, trying to turn my logic around on me. "We haven't known each other long enough for me to share such things."

Her face brightened. "Exactly. You have secrets, just like I do, but it doesn't have to change things between us."

"What you did changes *everything*." But she was right —the welfare of my employees and patients had to take priority over my emotions. "I'll give you two days or until I find your replacement."

"You won't be sorry."

"I already am."

15

$\mathcal{N}$ight fell thick and unshakable as I returned to the penthouse, mirroring my emotions. Ghost and Redemption greeted each other, and Corvus squawked a hello.

I hugged Redemption and stroked the raven's head, glad to be home and grateful for the glass of wine that Killion handed me.

A delicious aroma of food came from the kitchen. My stomach growled, and I took a big sip of wine. "I should have fired her."

He read my mind. "Your new office manager?"

I allowed him to lead me to the sofa. At least it was nice and cool in here. "She's a spy for SMG. Internal Affairs, checking up on me."

He considered me for a moment. "Did Death send her?"

I shook my head and petted Redemption. He put a paw in my lap. "Mei did. She's got a lot of guts. Death, too. He knew who Sylvie was and didn't warn me. Is it wrong that I want to kill both of them?"

Killion massaged the back of my neck. "Were you able to speak to Death about Mercer?"

"He denies there's anything going on with a curse or SMG using Mercer to do their dirty work. I don't know, I feel like he's playing his own game right now. Somebody's breathing down his neck to take care of the hunter, and he's putting pressure on me to carry it out."

"Sounds like they're all trying to control you," he said without nearly enough menace in his voice for my liking.

"Nothing new there, but it's not going to work. I *will* uncover the truth, save your vampire family, and send Sylvie packing."

"But first, dinner."

We rose, and he guided me to the dining room. There, he refilled my glass and poured himself one.

"I won't let them win," I said. "Whoever's behind Silas's curse. Whoever has manipulated him into doing their dirty work, I'm going to expose them, even if it means going rogue."

"You're calling him by his first name now."

A statement, not a question. "I'm not cutting him slack for kidnapping the family, but I feel a weird kindred spirit in the fact that SMG has screwed him over."

"If he's telling the truth."

It was a big if, but my intuition told me he was.

Pennyworth began serving a Mexican dish, my favorite cilantro rice, and homemade tortilla chips. There was also fresh guacamole.

"I don't care what Death, Mei, or Sylvie want," I said around a mouthful. It was so good, I could barely stop shoveling the dip and chips into my mouth to moan in pleasure. "I'm getting to the bottom of all of this."

"I would expect nothing less," Killion replied, a barely there smile tugging at his luscious lips.

Over our meal, I told him about the parasite outbreak. Nita had once more agreed to hang out with our overnight guests so I could get some rest. I owed her a gift card to her favorite spa.

On the way home, I'd texted Aurora and Andy, explaining the spreading problem to them. As Killion and I were finishing our meal, they arrived, and Penny-worth ushered them in.

Aurora looked as tired as I felt. "Need a drink?" I asked.

"Try several," she muttered, stepping past Andy to a dining room chair. She sank into it, setting a stack of leather-bound books next to the plate Pennyworth set in front of her. She thanked him and began filling it with food.

Andy took the chair next to her and did the same. Killion got up to get both of them glasses of wine.

"I brought everything I could find on magical rashes," she said after downing half of her wine. "There isn't much."

Not the answer I was hoping for. "Got anything to help me take revenge on my office manager?"

Andy glanced at me from his hunched position over his food. "The new gal? What did she do?"

"She's a mole," Killion answered for me.

I slugged back some wine, feeling it ease the tension in my shoulders. "She's internal affairs."

"Your employer has internal affairs?" At my nod, Andy grinned. "They waited long enough to turn you in."

I tossed my napkin at him. "According to Death, I'm the reason they now have the department. He thinks Silas is making it up about the curse, by the way. I couldn't convince him otherwise."

"Silas, huh?" Aurora didn't miss that I had used his first name. I waved it off, and she pushed a book toward me, its spine cracked with age. "I have a theory regarding the curse and the rash."

I flipped the volume open to where one of her sticky notes pointed to her research. "Go on."

"There are a few curses that cause odd side effects." She broke a chip in half, munching on the still-warm treat. She used the other piece to point at the page. "Since he claims to have been cursed for a while, and he's been dabbling in black magic, it's possible he's attracting the parasites to him. They're latching onto animals because the curse is repelling them once they get to Mercer. It's a Catch-22. The parasites are leeches who are drawn to the energy of the curse, but are also kept from the host by it. Does that make sense?"

"Sort of." She'd underlined a few phrases on the page, and I read those to deepen my understanding. "The curse is powerful black magic, which attracts them, but because of the equally powerful black magic Silas is using, it's creating an invisibility cloak they can't latch onto."

She nodded and swallowed another bite. "You haven't noticed any humans with the rash, have you?"

I shook my head. "And let's hope none of them come down with it. Any chance you have a remedy?"

"Working on that." She fished a plastic zippered bag from her pocket and slid it across the table. "This is to protect you. Two cups daily until we know what we're dealing with."

"Ugh, not another tea," I groaned.

"Hey." Her Irish accent sharpened, and Andy became overly interested in his food. "My teas have saved you more than once."

"True." I forced a smile. "Thank you."

We spent the next hour discussing Silas, the curse, the rash, and the missing couple. I volunteered to walk between worlds again and see if I could once more find the hunter and the essence he had deposited there to keep himself invisible. No one would take me up on it.

There was a time when I would have struck out on my own and done it anyway. The fact that I was so exhausted that I fell asleep at the table kept me from doing so.

Killion carted me off to bed, and I barely had the energy to argue.

I WOKE to a black feathered menace dive bombing my face, the insistent squawking of the avian alarm clock piercing through the last dregs of sleep. "I'm awake. I'm awake." I pushed Corvus off the pillow as he gave me a look that clearly said even dead people got up faster than I did.

A hot shower promised a shield from him, if not some semblance of clarity. Ghost pranced around my feet as I made my way to the bathroom, her energy a stark contrast to my morning lethargy.

The bathroom vanity held a steaming cup of coffee. "At least one of us is excited for today," I said, giving the dog a half-hearted pat as I avoided my reflection in the mirror.

Turning on the shower as hot as I could stand it, I downed half the coffee and brightened somewhat when Killion's magic flowed into the space right before he did. He didn't ask how I was, but took the cup from my hand, peeled off my nightgown, and joined me under the spray.

The water pounded away the remnants of sleep and some of my remaining frustration over the previous day's events. The nerves in my stomach proved more resilient, even as my husband washed my hair and used my favorite body wash to scrub me from top to bottom. I lingered in his arms as Death's warnings and his ultimatum echoed in my head. They mingled with Sylvie's casual betrayal and the supernatural parasites.

Under Killion's ministrations, the worst of it was pushed aside as I gave myself to him. His hands, mouth, and magic worked wonders on recharging my energy in a way that no amount of caffeine could do.

Once dressed and somewhat calmer, I made my way to the kitchen. Killion had beaten me there, a vision of early morning perfection. He handed me a fresh cup of coffee, and Pennyworth laid an omelet on a plate for me. I took both and went to the dining room to wolf them down.

Killion joined me with his own cup. "You slept well?"

I stared at his lips, the recent memory of where they

had been making my skin tingle. "Seems like it, but I don't feel any more rested. I kept having dreams about Death firing me. Which,"—I checked my watch—"is a strong possibility. I have approximately eight hours before his deadline is up to prove he's wrong and stop Silas from being a scapegoat for some master conspiracy. If there is one. Meanwhile, I have to disinfect the entire clinic due to the parasites and locate the missing family."

Killion's fingers interlaced with mine. "I'll be with you every step of the way. All will work out."

"I wish I were as sure as you. Another thing I need to do is keep Sylvie from reporting my actions back to SMG. I should fire her, but I think I may try to turn her to my cause." I'd come up with the idea when I'd been planning how to do the same with Silas.

One of his beautiful eyebrows quirked. "How?"

"She's already part of the insider group at SMG, and she admitted yesterday that she likes working at the clinic. If Death won't help me uncover who's behind the deal they made with Silas, maybe she will."

He tapped his temple with a finger and winked. "Smart."

"It probably won't work. She's trouble. More than I can afford right now, but if I could use her as a double agent, it would be a game changer."

"It's brilliant, and I have faith that you can do it. Exposing Mercer's blackmailer, who may also be involved in creating souls such as Diego to use as their personal army, is a good strategy. As per normal, you are fair and just. I believe you're more principled than most reapers."

I finished off my omelet and coffee. "Yet, I always end up in trouble. Why is that?"

He smiled, settling back in his chair. "I believe your moral code is working out for you better than you realize. That's the real reason SMG hasn't fired you. Mei Han has come to accept that no matter how irritating you are to her, you always do the right thing."

My phone dinged with a text from JR. I wiped my hands on my napkin and rose. "Gotta run. Everyone is pitching in with the clinic sanitization before we open."

Killion walked me to the door, where I gathered my things. "The hunt for the Aldrichs is stalled again. I will also help."

"Me, too," Pennyworth said, discarding his apron as he joined us. "Omwee and the others are already there."

I was grateful, especially since Pennyworth's partner rarely left the hotel. I'd never met anyone as introverted as Omwee. It meant a great deal to me that he would step out of his comfort zone to support me. "You didn't order him to do so, did you?" I asked Killion.

He feigned a hurt expression. "Would I do something like that?"

Pennyworth chuckled, opening the door for us. "Omwee volunteered. He thinks quite highly of you."

Since he'd once tried to kill me, I guess that was saying something. I squeezed Pennyworth's arm. "I'll make sure we get this over with as quickly as possible so he can return home."

If only I'd known then what awaited me and the others.

16

*K*illion and I walked through the front door of the clinic an hour before opening. The place was already lit up and lively. Sylvie stood in the waiting room with her hands on her hips as she doled out orders to JR, Nita, Mason, and Omwee like a drill sergeant.

Cleaning supplies and fresh boxes of face masks cluttered the front desk and made me wonder if I'd accidentally signed us all up for a biological warfare reenactment.

Maybe that's what we were facing, though.

I didn't know if a deep clean would be enough to stop whatever supernaturally-charged bug had gotten into the clinic. Sylvie didn't know either--I saw the uncertainty when she glanced away from me, suddenly focused on picking out a clean face mask for herself.

The sharp tang of disinfectant hit my nostrils, making my eyes water. Sylvie dropped to her hands and knees to scrub the reception floor, JR headed to the exam rooms to wipe down examination tables, and Nita attacked the waiting room chairs with spray bottles and paper towels.

"You guys are amazing," I said, reaching for a pair of gloves from the box on the desk.

Killion's phone rang, and he stepped outside to answer it.

Nita paused, blowing a strand of hair from her face. "After yesterday's nightmare, we aren't taking chances. Whatever this infection is, it's spreading fast."

JR emerged from exam room three, his Southern drawl seeming more pronounced due to fatigue. "Had four more calls last night from clients whose pets are showing symptoms. Something's seriously wrong, Chloey Bear."

It was rare for him to call me by that childhood nickname. A clear indication that he was already mentally exhausted by this issue. I was, too. I snapped on the gloves and grabbed a bottle of hospital-grade disinfectant. "We aren't going to let those little buggers win."

Mason, Pennyworth, and Omwee began methodically working through the supply cabinets, removing items, wiping down shelves, and replacing everything with meticulous care.

Killion returned, shaking his head at my silent question—no one had located Silas or the Aldrichs. He joined in the cleaning, rolling up his sleeves and helping me wipe down countertops.

While I worked, I let my grave sight slip into focus. The world transformed around me. Colors dimmed while supernatural energies became visible. I sucked in a sharp breath. What I saw made my stomach clench.

The parasites were *everywhere*.

They floated through the air like ghostly jellyfish, translucent and wispy with hundreds of hair-thin tendrils reaching hungrily toward anything living. Some merged into larger, pulsing masses that reminded me of spectral amoebas, spreading across the ceiling in patches of ethereal infection.

I shuffled through the clinic, noticing how they congregated densely around the exam tables where sick animals had been treated. They clung to surfaces despite the vigorous scrubbing.

I watched in horror as JR walked straight through a cluster of them, the parasites briefly disturbed by his passage before reforming. Several attached themselves to his lab coat without his realization. They didn't seem interested in him—they weren't latching onto his life force—but they were using him as transport, hitchhiking on his clothing.

"Hey, Chloe, you okay?" Sylvie's voice cut through my concentration.

I blinked, deactivating my grave sight. "Just thinking about which areas need the most attention."

Her serious, knowing look told me she suspected that was a lie. "From how pale you appear, I'd say all of them."

"You have no idea," I muttered. Killion joined us, his keen gaze locked on her. I suspected he was letting her know he didn't appreciate her betrayal of me. I spoke so that only the two of them would hear. "The parasites are still everywhere. The cleaning isn't working."

Killion frowned. "How bad?"

"Bad," I whispered, motioning them to follow me to

the back. "They're just too numerous, and they're adapting. Clustering together, changing shape, finding new ways to spread."

Sylvie's expression remained neutral, but I caught the flicker of concern in her eyes. "Maybe we need a different approach."

My attention was drawn to Nita, who was now cleaning the ultrasound machine. A quick glimpse through my grave sight revealed parasites swarming the equipment, eagerly reaching for her.

I hurried over. "Let me get that." I took the cleaning cloth from her hands. "Why don't you help JR?"

She gave me a curious look. "You sure? I was just about to—"

"Positive," I interrupted.

As soon as she left, I attacked the ultrasound machine with vigor. The parasites swirled away from my cloth only to return seconds later, unaffected by the chemicals that would have killed any earthly contaminant.

I felt a hand on my shoulder. Killion met my gaze as I swiveled to look at him. *This isn't working.*

A weight settled in my chest, an uncomfortable heaviness. *What should I do?*

But I knew.

I had to close the clinic.

The unfairness of it hit me like a physical blow. This was supernatural in origin—my territory as a grim reaper —yet it affected the normal, everyday world I'd fought hard to maintain alongside my supernatural responsibilities. The worlds were colliding in the worst possible way, and innocent animals were caught in the crossfire.

The clinic had been my parents' legacy, and dreaming of it becoming mine after their deaths had been my lifeline during the darkest time of my life. The thought of closing its doors, even temporarily, felt like losing them all over again.

My fingers curled against the ultrasound machine, my knuckles whitening beneath the blue nitrile gloves. Killion's hand continued to rest on my shoulder. With a heavy sigh, I pulled off the gloves and tossed them into the biohazard bin. "Everyone," I called, my voice steadier than I felt. "Can we gather in the break room? There's something we need to discuss."

Killion gave me an almost imperceptible nod of approval. It didn't make what I had to do any easier, but at least I wasn't facing it alone.

Once everyone was there, I stood at the head of our cramped break room table, all eyes fixed on me with expressions ranging from curiosity to concern. The words "we need to close the clinic" sat heavy on my tongue, reluctant to be spoken aloud. My parents had never closed the doors, even during the worst blizzard in the town's history, and here I was, about to announce a shutdown because of something I couldn't even explain to most of the people in the room. The irony of being able to see death but not prevent it twisted like a knife in my chest.

Killion leaned against the wall, his presence reassuring despite the difficulty of what I needed to say. Sylvie offered a subtle nod of encouragement. At least two people in the room understood the full picture.

I took a deep breath. "Based on what we're seeing with these infections, we need to close temporarily."

The reaction was immediate and exactly what I expected.

"Close?" JR's voice rose sharply. "We've got twenty-seven appointments scheduled for today alone."

I held up my hand. "I know, and—"

"The Henderson's German Shepherd is coming in for his hip evaluation," JR continued, as if I hadn't spoken. "We've been monitoring him for weeks. And Mrs. Pavelski's rescue cats need their follow-up vaccines. Ms. Hemsworth is bringing in that parrot. We already put her off from Friday."

Each name felt like an individual weight added to my shoulders. These weren't just appointments; they were living beings who depended on us.

"What about the antibiotics we started Bella on yesterday?" Nita chimed in. "Her owners can't travel to the next county for a follow-up. They're elderly."

"And the Johnsons' puppy," Mason added quietly. "The one that nearly died from parvo last week. He's supposed to come in for a checkup."

I rubbed my temples. "I understand all of that, but—"

"We're disinfecting everything," Nita pressed. "I mean, look at us—we're practically swimming in bleach."

"The disinfection isn't working," I said, and added a small lie. "I just took some scrapings from various spots we've cleaned. The parasites are still there. Whatever this is, it's immune to our efforts. If we don't close, we risk more animals becoming infected."

JR crossed his arms, the scar above his eyebrow that

I'd given him long ago when we were kids becoming more pronounced. "Chloe, with all due respect, closing isn't the answer. Where will these animals go? The nearest clinic is thirty miles away, and from what Lincoln told me at church yesterday, they're overwhelmed with patients just like we are."

Lincoln was a fellow vet who worked in a neighboring town.

"I know," I said, feeling increasingly trapped. "But you haven't seen—" I caught myself before saying they hadn't seen the parasites floating through the air, attaching themselves to everything living. "Containment is our only ethical option. You saw how fast Markem went down once he was infected."

Nita's expression softened from argumentative to one of concern. "Look, I get that you're worried. We all are. But these animals need us. Your parents would never—"

"Don't." The word came out sharper than I intended. "Please don't tell me what my parents, who never had to deal with something like this, would have done."

The room went silent. I was trying to protect the clinic they'd built, and that had hit a nerve.

"I'm sorry," Nita said quietly. "That wasn't fair."

I took a deep breath, let it go softly. "It's okay. I'm not making this decision lightly, but I have reason to believe that continuing normal operations puts every animal that comes through our doors at risk."

"What reason?" JR challenged. "Because right now it sounds like you're overreacting to a few cases of an unusual infection."

He'd always been stubborn.

I stood firm, knowing how inadequate my arguments sounded. "I have information you don't."

His lips pressed into an unforgiving line. "That's not good enough. We're a team. If you know something about what's happening, we all deserve to hear it."

Killion tensed. The air in the room thickened. Pennyworth and Omwee exchanged uncomfortable glances while Nita looked torn between supporting me and agreeing with JR.

"It's complicated," I said.

"Uncomplicate it," JR insisted. "Because right now, you're asking us to turn away sick animals without a solid explanation."

Sylvie slid up beside me. "She told you—she checked the areas we've cleaned, and the parasites are still active. That should be enough to convince you that we need to close temporarily until we can figure this out."

"Chloe's right," Killion added. "We don't know what we're dealing with. Until we do, the clinic has a responsibility not to exacerbate the issue."

The weight of dual responsibilities—to the supernatural world and my clinic—was suffocating. This was the eternal struggle of my existence: living between worlds, belonging fully to neither.

As a grim reaper, I had a duty to contain supernatural threats. As a veterinarian, I had sworn to heal and protect. Now those paths had collided, and I couldn't navigate both without revealing secrets that weren't mine to share.

"What if we compromise?" All heads turned toward Sylvie.

"What kind of compromise?" I asked.

"Instead of closing completely, what if we create a quarantine system?" she suggested. "We only accept animals already showing symptoms of the infection—essentially becoming a treatment center for the issue."

There was no treatment yet, but our eyes met, and I caught her subtle message: this would allow us to monitor the supernatural infection while still providing care.

"We could convert the back into a treatment area," she continued. "Full isolation protocols. Separate ventilation, if possible. Monitor all the cases."

"Harlow could assist with the vaccinations and follow-ups of the non-infected," Killion volunteered. "If there are patients who need rides to another clinic, I will hire people to take care of them."

Mason nodded. "Mom will be glad to help out."

Not. Harlow was going to hate me.

JR's rigid posture eased slightly. "That could work."

"We can reschedule routine appointments and wellness visits." Nita warmed to the idea. "But we could help the animals that are already sick."

"And potentially study what's happening," Sylvie added, "so we can better understand how to treat it."

She'd found the middle ground I couldn't see, a solution that acknowledged both my supernatural concerns and my veterinary obligations.

"It would mean strict adherence to quarantine procedures," I cautioned.

"We can handle it," JR said, his earlier opposition gone. "If it means staying open for the animals that need us most, we'll make it work."

I looked around the table, seeing renewed purpose in my team's expressions. The tension in the room had transformed into something productive, a shared mission rather than a divided one.

"Okay," I agreed, relieved. "Let's do it. Quarantine protocols for infected animals only. We'll call and reschedule all routine appointments, and for those who need check-ups or vaccinations, we'll rely on Harlow."

"I'll handle the rescheduling," Sylvie said.

"I'll set up the isolation zone," JR added. "We've got those plastic barrier sheets we used during the renovations last year. We can create a physical separation."

As everyone began discussing logistics, I caught Sylvie's eye and mouthed a silent "thank you." She gave me a smile in return, the kind that acknowledged our shared secret.

Ugh. I didn't want to like her, but I did.

Killion moved closer as the others continued planning. "Crisis somewhat averted," he murmured in my ear.

"But it doesn't solve the actual problem."

"No," he agreed, "but it buys us time to find a solution without abandoning your professional responsibilities."

I felt relief at the compromise, gratitude for allies who understood my dual nature, and lingering anxiety about the parasites still floating through my clinic. *It's a bandage on a bullet wound.*

Perhaps, he replied through our connection, *but even*

immortals must sometimes address the immediate crisis before solving the greater problem.

It wasn't perfect, but straddling two worlds rarely allowed for perfection.

17

*W*hile I was checking on our patients, Killion cleared his throat. The sound, though quiet, commanded immediate attention. "Perhaps," he suggested, "we could all use some fortification. Drinks and pastries would provide a welcome boost, would they not? JR and Nita, could you run to The Bean and procure some for us?"

JR checked his watch, frowning. "We've got a lot to do before—"

"My treat," Killion interrupted, pulling out his wallet and extracting several crisp bills. His violet eyes flicked to me briefly, and I caught the subtle message: he needed them gone. Now. "For everyone's dedication this morning. A small token of appreciation."

Nita brightened. "The maple scones should be fresh out of the oven, and I could use the caffeine." JR hesitated, but she grabbed his arm. "Come on, we can use your car. It'll take fifteen minutes, tops."

"Get my usual?" I asked, playing along.

As soon as the door closed behind them, the atmosphere in the clinic shifted. Mason, Pennyworth, and Omwee gathered around us. Sylvie cocked a brow.

"What I'm about to attempt may not work," Killion said, "but I need to try it without the non-magicals around."

"What are you planning?" I asked, following him as he strode purposefully toward the kennels and our infected patients.

"A direct approach," he replied. "These parasites are supernatural, which means conventional methods are useless. However, they might respond to a certain *type* of magic."

"Like what, Master?" Pennyworth asked.

"My particular brand."

Mason's eyes widened. "Your dragon magic?"

Killion nodded. "It's not without risk. This level of power is... noticeable. It will send ripples throughout the supernatural community."

"But it might work?" I pressed.

"We shall see." He glanced at Pennyworth and Omwee. "Secure the perimeter. No interruptions." His intense and reproachful gaze slid to Sylvie. "This isn't SMG business. You should leave."

The vampires nodded and took positions by the front and rear exits. Mason backed up a few steps.

Sylvie moved beside me, curious but cautious. "An infectious parasite caused by supernatural causes and affecting this world *is* my business, regardless of who my employer is. I'll stay, thank you."

Killion's heavy gaze landed on me to see what I wanted. I shrugged. "Let her stay."

He stood in the center of the main treatment area, closed his eyes, and extended his arms. For a moment, nothing happened.

Then, the air around him began to shimmer like heat waves rising from hot summer pavement. His breathing deepened, eventually each exhale carrying a faint, barely perceptible wisp of smoke.

When he opened his eyes, his irises blazed red with inner fire. Veins of orange light appeared beneath his skin, tracing intricate scale patterns up his arms like luminous tattoos etched in living flame.

He raised his hands, a bright light swirling in his palms. The glow intensified until it hurt to look directly at it, casting dramatic shadows across the clinic's white walls. With a fluid gesture, he sent the first pulse of energy outward.

The wave expanded in a perfect arc, passing through solid objects as if they weren't there. It raised the tiny hairs on the back of my neck, and my inner fire responded, leaping to connect with it. I activated my grave sight in time to see the wave hit the first cluster of soul parasites.

The effect was immediate and dramatic. They shriveled on contact, their wispy tendrils curling inward like burning paper. They seemed to scream, though no sound reached my physical ears—just a psychic impression of agony that made me wince.

Moments before, they'd been floating, crawling, predatory entities. Now, they collapsed into themselves, disintegrating into specks of ghostly ash that dissipated into nothingness.

Killion sent another pulse, stronger than the first. My magic ached from it as it rippled outward in a dome shape, catching parasites hiding in ceiling corners and air vents. They withered by the dozens, then hundreds.

"It's working," I breathed, turning in a circle to watch the destruction. "Killion, it's working!"

He didn't respond, his concentration absolute as he gathered more power between his hands. The fiery light condensed into a sphere of pure energy. Mason and Sylvie gaped, but neither seemed affected. Sweat beaded on his forehead. His jaw clenched with concentration. The veins of light beneath his skin pulsed, making the scales more vivid. The temperature in the room rose steadily as the air conditioner hummed to life.

With a gesture that reminded me of a conductor leading an orchestra, he flung tendrils of it into every corner of the clinic, guiding them with precise movements.

The display was beautiful and terrifying—raw power controlled with deadly precision. They snaked through the building, seeking parasites like hounds on a scent trail. When they found their targets, they burned them out of existence.

When it was over, the light receded gradually, retreating into his body until only his eyes retained the red glow. He took a deep, steadying breath, and even that simple action seemed to cost him effort.

"I believe the main areas are clear," he said, his voice

rough. "We should check the infected animals while my senses are still heightened."

I led him to Markem's isolation kennel. The Irish setter lay on a comfortable bed, an IV providing fluids and medication. I could still see parasites clinging to the dog, though they seemed sluggish.

Killion opened the kennel door and knelt beside it, placing one hand near but not touching the dog's body. His eyes remained violet but took on a brighter than normal shine as he studied the parasites through whatever senses his dragon provided.

"Fascinating," he murmured. "They've integrated with his life force in a way I've not seen before. It's systematic."

"Can you help him?" I asked.

"Perhaps." Killion extended his hand, allowing a gentle form of the orange light to emanate from his fingertips. It enveloped Markem, and the dog's breathing, which had been shallow and labored, deepened and steadied.

The parasites reacted, recoiling, but seemed unable to detach completely from their host. They writhed in apparent distress, their tendrils flailing uselessly.

"They resist," Killion observed. "They've established a connection that makes complete removal difficult without risking damage to the host."

Disappointment sent my stomach falling. "So you can't cure him?"

"Let's find out. Before I attempt a full cleansing, I need to understand their nature better." He frowned, studying the parasites with intense concentration.

"There's something curious about them that..." His words trailed off.

Abruptly, he straightened. "Silas Mercer," he said, the name falling from his lips like a revelation.

"What about him?".

Killion's eyes met mine, urgency in his expression. "Do you remember what he said about his curse?"

I tried to recall his exact phrasing. "He said something about being forced to destroy supernatural communities..." I got it then. "He said it was *systematic*."

"Systematic," Killion repeated. "These parasites attach to their hosts in a systematic pattern—the physical form, then the life force. And they spread systematically, starting with the weakest links in a community—animals. What do you want to bet that they eventually spread to other beings?"

Understanding dawned on me. "We assumed they were connected to his curse."

"Not simply connected," Killion said gravely. "I believe they may be manifestations of the curse itself. Physical and metaphysical—embodiments of the destructive force that compels him."

The implication hit me. "So when we're fighting these parasites..."

"We're fighting aspects of that curse," Killion finished. "And if that's true, eradicating them might weaken or even break the curse itself."

Hope surged. "Your dragon magic can destroy them."

"Yes," he agreed, "but not without cost. You saw how many there were, how quickly they reproduce and spread. Cleansing the entire town would require more power than I can safely channel."

"But you could cleanse individual animals?" I pressed. "Like Markem?"

Killion contemplated the dog. "Possibly. And perhaps with practice, I could develop a more efficient approach."

The sound of a car pulling into the rear parking lot interrupted us.

Mason peered through the blinds. "It's JR and Nita," he reported. "They're back."

Killion closed his eyes briefly, the last traces of light fading as he composed himself.

"We need to locate Silas Mercer again," I said before they entered.

Killion nodded. "Agreed. And if my theory is correct, ending this infection might not only save your patients but also free him from his curse."

The door opened, bringing the scent of coffee and pastries, and with it, the return to our human façades.

But beneath the surface, things had changed. We now had a theory and a potential solution.

"I need to step out for a bit," I told my friends as I accepted a coffee.

To my relief, JR nodded. "We can handle things."

"Full PPE protocols—gloves, gowns, foot covers. Change between patients. And—" I hesitated, trying to phrase the next part carefully, "—call me immediately if you notice anything unusual. Anything at all, no matter how strange it seems."

Nita bit into a scone. "Define unusual."

I felt a pang of guilt for keeping her in the dark about

the supernatural nature of the threat. She deserved the truth, but telling her would drag her into a world that often proved dangerous for humans with that knowledge. "Trust your instincts. You're good at what you do. If something feels off, it probably is. When Dr. O'Leary arrives, bring him up to speed."

Sylvie was taking notes, her neat handwriting filling a page with instructions. "And we're still rescheduling all wellness visits?"

"Absolutely," I confirmed. "No healthy animals in the building if we can help it. I'll be back as soon as I can. I need to follow up on a potential source of the infection. Killion's coming with me."

"A source?" JR perked up. "You mean you know where this is coming from?"

"I have a theory. Nothing concrete yet, but worth investigating."

"Take your time," Sylvie said meaningfully. "We can handle things."

I gathered my jacket and bag. Killion had already stepped outside, likely alerting Harlow and Katarina to our mission.

"Ready?" he asked when I joined him. The limo idled at the curb.

"Almost." I turned back toward the clinic. "I just want to make sure—"

My words died as the sound of screeching tires cut through the morning air.

Aurora skidded to a stop in her tiny, white electric car, leaping out, her usually composed demeanor replaced by pure panic. "Chloe!" she shouted. "Help!"

My stomach dropped as I recognized Andy slumped in the passenger seat. The wolf shifter looked terribly wrong—his tan skin was ashen, his lanky frame bent forward as if in pain. Aurora struggled to drag him out of the vehicle.

Killion moved with supernatural speed, reaching Andy before I could take two steps.

"What happened?" I demanded. "What's wrong?"

Aurora grabbed a bag from the back as Killion helped Andy exit the car. Andy groaned, his head lolling to one side. "Tried...to shift," he managed, his voice rough like sandpaper. "Couldn't complete it."

Aurora grabbed my arm, her fingers digging through my jacket. "I think he's infected."

My stomach somersaulted. "The parasites?"

Her nod made the world swim under my feet. I placed my hand on Andy's forehead, feeling the unnatural chill of his skin. This was deeply concerning for a wolf shifter who normally ran several degrees hotter than humans. My grave sight instinctively kicked in. Aurora was right— he was infected, and it was bad. Really bad.

"I can't take him to the hospital," she said. "They're more likely to kill him than help him."

"You're sure about the cause?" Killion asked.

I swallowed the lump in my throat, keeping the horror off my face as I nodded. I had no words.

My mate glanced at the clinic and then back at Andy. With the humans inside, we couldn't explain Andy being a shifter or why taking him to a human hospital would do no good.

"They're morphing. No one is safe," I said. "Not

shifters, not witches—" A terrible thought struck me. "Not even vampires."

The implications hung between us. Andy pushed away from Killion. "Oh, crud. I hadn't thought of that."

He staggered, and we all reached for him. Killion ordered Andy to put his arm around his neck. "They will not harm me because of my dragon."

My grave sight showed that none of us were carriers at the moment. Was Andy an easy target for them because of his animalistic nature? I offered my theory to the others.

"Makes sense," Aurora said, "but what do we do?"

What had started as an infection among animals had become a potential threat to the entire supernatural community of Danté's Grove. The devastation would be unimaginable if these parasites could adapt to different supernatural physiologies.

"We need to find Mercer," Killion said. "Now more than ever."

"First, you have to heal him." I peeked at the clinic window, where Sylvie was watching. "Let's take him to the church."

Aurora glanced at Killion. "You can do that? Heal him?"

"Maybe," he said. "I can kill the parasites, it seems."

She looked relieved. "Thank the goddess."

Andy groaned and grabbed his stomach.

"We'll take him with us," I told Aurora. "You follow. We need to go. Now."

Before we could pull out, a man in a duster with a black mastiff came walking down the sidewalk.

18

I jumped from the limo in a heartbeat, marching for Silas Mercer. He and the mastiff pulled up short as I pointed a finger at him and then at the car. "Get in."

Sylvie emerged from the clinic, rushing toward me. "Is that him? The hunter?"

"I'm handling it," I told her. "Go back inside."

"You have to reap him," she ordered.

My burning grim tattoo and itching palm agreed.

"I felt an abnormal wave of magic a minute ago." His sullen gaze bounced to her. "You from SMG?" He didn't wait for her answer. "Just stay out of this."

Her hands went to her hips. "I will not. You're Chloe's assignment." She pinned me with a glare. "Get your scythe and reap him."

The smiling, always pleasant woman had morphed into a mini-Death. "He's directly connected to the missing vampire family," I told her. "If I kill him, they die. Their daughter is human, and none of their soul contracts are up."

She started to retort, probably to remind me that vampires forfeited their soul contract when they elected to be turned, but then shifted her focus. "What have you done?" she asked Silas.

He rocked back, narrowing his eyes at her. "What have *I* done? What has your employer done? They've screwed me over a dozen different ways, including the curse they put on me. So, pack up your self-righteousness and get out of my face."

She made a noise that sounded as if he'd slapped her. "I've seen your record. I know you're a rogue. The damage you have done on this earth is horrible. Hunting supernaturals without reason or cause, and creating universal imbalance everywhere you go. Don't you dare act high and mighty to me."

He hitched a thumb toward her as he asked me, "Who is she and what's she doing here?"

"Sylvie Pearson," she told him. "And I'm here to make sure Chloe does her job."

He snorted without looking at her. "Got them looking over your shoulder, have you, reaper?"

Sylvie stepped forward and began yelling at him again. I grabbed her arm and pulled her back. "I know a way to break the curse."

His eyes widened, and his mocking tone disappeared. "How?"

Sylvie whipped her head toward me. "What are you talking about? *There is no curse.* Death said he's making that up."

The mastiff sniffed me. I could see the parasites attached to him. It was everything I could do not to jerk Sylvie away and have Killion blast the dog. "There's more going on here than we're being told," I said to her. "Until you have the full story, don't assume you know the truth."

Silas gave a nod, as if I had taken his side. "Yeah, you can go back to SMG and tell them to go to—"

I cut him off. "She's not going anywhere." His expression turned hard again. I continued. "Your curse has contaminated our town. Parasites are rapidly infesting animals, and now,"—I pointed toward the limo—"a wolf shifter. It won't be long before they're everywhere, affecting mortals and supernaturals alike. You're both going to help me stop this and save innocent lives."

"Parasites?" Silas made a face. His gaze dropped to the dog. "What's that got to do with the curse?"

"Everything. See that white car behind the limo? You and your dog are going to hitch a ride with the witch who's driving it. Do not piss her off, or you'll have worse things to worry about than my blade ending your sorry existence. We're going to get this straightened out, and it starts with you."

He balked, and Sylvie argued, yelling over him. Even the mastiff started barking, adding to the uproar.

A sharp whistle pierced the air, silencing all three. We turned in unison to see Killion beside the limo with a scowl resembling a summer storm. "You'll do as Chloe says."

The reverberation of the command carried the same intensity as the scowl. It was only a few notches down from the dragon power he'd unleashed inside the clinic.

The mastiff dropped to his belly and whimpered. Silas's shoulders drooped. Sylvie shuddered. With her back ramrod straight, she walked toward the limo. "I'm going with you."

"I need you to stay here and take care of the clinic," I told her. "This isn't up for negotiation. Either you help me, or you call Death and tell him you failed to keep me in line. What's it going to be?"

Anger simmered in her eyes, but she realized I had her in a bind. "Keep me posted." She checked her watch and flicked a hateful glare at Silas. "You have seven hours, Chloe. Make them count."

She disappeared inside, and I gestured for Silas and the dog to get in Aurora's car. Through the windshield, I could see my friend wasn't excited about the arrangement, and she was none too happy that we'd been interrupted to begin with. She rolled down her window and yelled, "Can we go now? Andy doesn't have much time."

When we got to the church, Katarina was there to meet us. As Killion's enforcer, she lived there and conducted some of his business. Whether it was interrogations or training, she ruled supreme between the stained glass windows and ancient stone walls.

She had two ghost dogs I had accidentally resurrected before my necromancy abilities were under control. They tended to play and sleep in the cemetery, and when we arrived, they came barreling toward us. I called to her to keep them away, and she sent a silent message to them that had them scurrying back to the cemetery.

Getting Andy inside was no small feat. Once we

entered the nave, where the torture instruments took up more space than the remaining pews, Killion and Silas got him on a table.

The mastiff sniffed at an old blood stain on the floor, while Aurora stood at Andy's head and chanted a spell over him. Killion placed restraints around Andy's wrists and ankles.

Aurora paused. "Are those necessary?"

Andy groaned as Killion finished with the last one and ordered Katarina to bring him some blood. "I don't know how he'll react to what I'm about to do. Better safe than sorry."

"You never told me how you're going to break this curse," Silas said to me.

Katarina returned with the blood in a fancy goblet, and Killion downed it. I jutted my chin toward the master vampire, who closed his eyes. "Watch."

Just like at the clinic, the air around him began to shimmer. His deepening exhales brought up smoke.

When he opened his eyes, they burned red. The veins of orange light appeared beneath his skin, lighting up the faint outline of his scales.

Silas gasped. Katarina smiled. The mastiff cocked his head.

"Should I stay here?" Aurora whispered to me.

She wasn't infected. Yet. I gestured for her to join me and Katarina out of the line of fire.

The giant statue of St. Ann looked down on us with vacant eyes from her place on the dais. She'd been blasted apart and repaired the previous year, and never wavered in her surveillance of the things that went on here.

Killion raised his hands, that ball of light swirling in his palms. With a fluid gesture, he sent a wave of energy toward Andy.

The wave wrapped the shifter in a bubble, and he jerked. His teeth clinched, and he growled low in his throat, the muscles straining as his head snapped back.

Aurora started to go to him, but Katarina and I held her back. Killion injected a second wave of light into the bubble. Andy howled.

I wrapped an arm around Aurora's shoulders as she winced. I activated my grave sight, praying it would show me what I wanted to see.

The parasites were burning. That was the good thing.

Andy's wolf essence was burning, too. Not so good.

He spasmed and gripped the table, his body trembling.

Silas watched with horrified eyes.

Aurora shot out a hand. "Stop! Please, Killion! It's killing him!"

Not him, I told Killion through our channel. *Just his wolf.*

What would Andy be without his shifter magic? Once you've had magic, you can't imagine a life without it. It becomes as much a part of you as one of your limbs, your brain, your very breath.

But if we didn't do this, he could die.

Killion decreased the light but didn't stop. Andy's body relaxed a fraction, drool trickling from the corners of his mouth. His voice came out ragged and haunting. "Don't...stop..."

Killion switched from a constant stream of light to pulses—one...two...three...with subtle breaks between them. Each time one hit, Andy convulsed. When it receded, his body relaxed.

"It's working," I said, watching the predatory entities collapse and disintegrate into specks of ghostly ash. "Hang in there, Andy."

When it was done, the shifter was decontaminated. Unfortunately, he was no longer a shifter.

He sat in a pew, hanging his head, a blanket around his shoulders.

Aurora cried softly as she cradled him to her. Katarina, rarely moved my displays of emotion, left the room.

Silas petted the mastiff, a shocked expression on his face.

"He's next," Killion said, drinking more blood and adjusting his rolled-up shirt sleeves.

Silas paled. "Me?"

"The dog," I said, grabbing the leash. "Come on, big boy."

We could not lift the massive dog onto the table, so I tied him to it instead. He whined and looked at Silas.

The hunter nervously patted his head. "It's okay, buddy. Everything's going to be okay." Silas's eyes met mine. "Right? You're going to save him?"

Behind the question was another. *You're going to save me, right?*

"Yes," I told him, hoping it was true, but I already

knew there was no saving the thing masquerading as a dog. "We're going to do our best to save the innocent."

Killion finished off his blood. "Tell me where the family is first."

Silas shrank back. "Heal the dog, then I'll tell you."

"That's not how this works," my husband said. "You're lucky I don't kill you both right here, right now. I suspect Cormac and Roma are already too far gone to be saved, but I'm giving you this one chance to relieve your conscience and do the right thing."

"I don't have a conscience," Silas replied. His tone was matter-of-fact. "Lost it when my family was tortured and killed."

Killion stood his ground. "Your fight is with SMG, not me or the Aldrichs. If you want revenge, work with us to expose the corruption. Break free of the curse and see what justice you can get for your loved ones."

Silas was spiteful but not stupid. It was the best deal he was going to get. "How do I know you aren't a lying piece of—"

Killion's eyes flashed red. "Consider your next words carefully. You don't want me as your enemy."

"You already are, aren't you?"

"Regardless of what you claim will happen to the Aldrichs if I kill you, you won't walk out of here alive if you don't give me what I want."

Silas took in the torture devices, St. Ann, me. I held my tongue, sensing that Killion wasn't bluffing.

Katarina stuck her head in. "Found them, Master!"

Killion smiled—a brutal, confident thing that sent

shivers down my spine. "We don't need you anymore, Mercer."

He raised his hands as if to blast Silas with his magic, and the man recoiled, lifting both hands. "No, wait! Don't kill me!"

Killion didn't listen.

The blast knocked Silas to the floor, his body convulsing as he was struck by dragon fire.

19

"Stop!" Sylvie rushed in, waving her hands in the air. "He's Chloe's kill, not yours!"

Guess I shouldn't have been surprised that Sylvie had followed us after all.

Killion ignored her.

I have a plan to flush out whoever cursed him at SMG, I told Killion telepathically. *But I need Silas alive for it to work.*

Silas writhed on the floor, Killion's face alight with fury.

"Stop him!" Sylvie ordered me.

"You don't stop a vampire master," I told her. *Please,* I said to him.

The light dissipated. Killion dropped his hands. His eyes still showed red as he glared at me. "What is this plan?"

I helped Silas to a pew where he sank in a heap, panting. "When did you get the dog?" I asked him.

He barely glanced at me. "What?"

I pointed at the mastiff. "The dog. When you get him?"

He rubbed his forehead. "A couple of days after my family died. He showed up in my backyard."

I studied the animal. "He's not actually alive," I told everyone. "He's the curse."

Sylvie shook her head. "There is no curse, Chloe."

"There is, *Vi*," I said. "And that's what's causing the parasites. We destroy the curse, which is in dog form, we permanently destroy the parasites."

All eyes went to the mastiff. Or the thing posing as it.

"You can't be serious," Sylvie said. "You're not going to kill that innocent animal."

"It's not an animal," I corrected. "It's a manifestation of the curse that SMG used to keep Silas in line. This ends here." I glanced at Killion. "I need my scythe."

I'd left it in the limo. He made for the exit to grab it.

"I don't believe it," Silas said, "and I'm with Sylvie. You can't kill Rufus. He saved me after what happened with my wife and son. If it wasn't for him..."

The dog-curse whined, sensing his impending doom.

"Believe me, I don't like it," I said, "but I can see the parasites. It took me a minute, but I just realized Rufus isn't real. He's just a...mass of cursed leeches."

Silas bolted to his feet, swaying slightly. "You're not killing him."

Sylvie stepped up beside him and said to me, "Surely, there's another way."

"Chloe's right," Aurora said from where she was propping up Andy. "Whoever cursed Silas used the dog to deliver said curse and keep it active."

"Stay out of this," Silas snarled.

Sylvie moved to shield the dog as Killion returned with my blade. "I need to contact SMG and see what my orders are. I command you to stand down until I can do so."

My tattoo heated, and my palm blazed. I accepted the scythe and rubbed the handle with my thumb. "I'm sorry, but that's not going to happen. Now, move."

She lifted her chin. "I will not. There has to be a better solution."

At least she wasn't yelling at me to kill Silas. "I think the real reason you're afraid to let me do this is because you know I'm right. There *is* a curse, and that means that SMG and Death have been lying to you."

Killion narrowed his eyes at her, understanding where I was going with all of this. "And you don't want us to kill the dog because you don't want the curse to be broken. You're in on it, aren't you, Sylvie, or whatever your real name is? You and Death, both."

"That's ridiculous," she said, smoothing her hands over her stomach. "You're trying to make me out to be a bad guy in order to cover for Chloe's ineptness."

My mouth fell open. "My *ineptness*? You did read my record, right? Do you know who I really am? What I've handled?"

"What I know is that you're a grim reaper who has gone rogue more than once," she replied tartly. "You're about to do the same again. I want to help you, Chloe, but your behavior is unacceptable."

I wanted to bang my head on the scythe. "In case this

wasn't in your report, I am Grim Zero. Did Mei or Death tell you that?"

Her face paled. It took her a few beats to wrap her mind around that. "They did not. However, that doesn't change anything."

"Of course it does. I've been dealing with life and death since the beginning of time. SMG keeps trying to put me in a box so they can control me, but it always backfires on them. I've seen how they manipulate and betray those they should be loyal to." I tapped the scythe against my leg. "How do we know you're not the person who cursed Silas to begin with?"

She blinked. "I would never do such a thing, nor would I be in cahoots with anyone who would."

"Prove it. Help me figure out who the culprit is."

She glanced at Silas, back to me and the scythe. "I need time to figure this out."

"We don't have time. The parasites are going to rip through this town and destroy innocent animals and supernaturals. You're trying to save one entity that isn't even real while placing all these other beings with souls in danger."

I stepped toward the dog, motioning for her to move aside. If she didn't, she was going to get caught in the crossfire, and while I might be sorry about it, in the end, I would not let her stop me.

She held up both hands, standing her ground. "I need to understand more about this curse."

"The time for that's done," I said, raising my weapon. "Move, or you're going down with it."

I was expecting her to try to stop me, but what happened next took me by surprise.

The world around me shifted, and I was transported to the in-between. The mastiff was no longer a dog.

It was the angry, chained monster connected to Silas, with claws and pointed teeth.

And it was bearing down on me.

20

I stood on ground that wasn't quite solid, facing a monster that wasn't quite corporeal.

My stomach twisted with a dread that was all too real. The Curse Creature towered before me, its form a churning mass of shadows bound by chains of pulsing, electric energy that crackled and hissed.

The air—if you could call it that—felt too thick, as if I was breathing through wet cotton. Sounds echoed strangely, sometimes reaching my ears seconds after they occurred, sometimes it seemed, before they happened.

Colors existed here that had no names in the human world, shimmering at the edges of my vision and disappearing whenever I tried to look directly at them.

The monster writhed against its bindings. Each chain anchored it to points in the misty, not-quite-ground beneath it. Its body shifted constantly, first appearing almost human-shaped, then sprawling outward. The only constant was the sense of malevolence it radiated. The void of darkness at its core emitted a hungry emptiness that made my skin crawl.

Getting close enough to use my scythe would be tricky, but I'd faced worse.

Or so I thought.

A familiar figure popped into existence between me and the monster, eyes wide with shock as she took in the impossible landscape around her.

"Sylvie?" I choked out. "What are you doing here?"

Seeing the monster, she stumbled back and turned toward me, her sundress rippling oddly in the non-existent breeze. A relieved smile spread across her face. "Chloe? Where are we?"

"You can't be here," I said, panic clogging my throat. "This is the realm between worlds."

The monster suddenly lunged, moving with a speed that defied its size. One moment, it was restrained by its chains; the next, it stretched, its form elongating to resemble dark ink poured through the air. Before I could shout a warning, before I could even move, it reached Sylvie.

A massive, shadowy appendage wrapped around her petite frame, yanking her off her feet and pulling her to the monster's torso. Her scream cut through the otherworldly silence, sharp, terrified, and horribly human.

"No!" I lunged, but I was too far away, too slow.

The creature's grip tightened around her midsection. Another smoky tendril formed what might have been a hand—if hands were made of living darkness and ended in talons that weren't quite solid. This new appendage seized Sylvie's head.

I was still screaming, still reaching for her when the monster twisted.

The crack that followed was one of the most awful sounds I'd ever heard—sharp, wet, and final. It echoed in the strange acoustics of the space, repeating itself on some hellish loop. Sylvie's body went limp, her head lolling at an impossible angle, eyes still open but suddenly empty, the light behind them snuffed out.

The thing released her, and she crumpled to the misty ground, a broken doll discarded by a cruel child. Her body settled, still and wrong in a way that made me vomit, her limbs splayed at unnatural angles, her face frozen in the last moment of shock.

I couldn't breathe and gagged again. I couldn't think. Sylvie, whom I'd just been talking to, dead. Murdered. Right in front of me.

My horror gave way to a fury so intense it felt like my blood had been replaced with lava, burning me from the inside out. My vision narrowed, focused solely on the creature that had just ended a life as carelessly as stepping on an ant.

A sound tore from my throat—not quite a scream, not quite a growl—as I clasped the scythe tightly. The familiar weight of it settled into my palm, the handle cool against my skin. "You're...done," I snarled, my words emerging broken and raw.

I charged, closing the distance between us with rage-fueled strides. The creature contorted, its form roiling. I swung the scythe in a wide arc, aiming for center mass.

The blade connected not with the monster itself, but with one of the chains binding it. Blue-white sparks erupted from the point of contact, showering me like a waterfall. The chain didn't break, but something else did—my grip.

The recoil was violent, the scythe handle wrenched from my grasp with such force that I felt something in my wrist tear. The weapon spun away, end over end, catching what little light existed in this place as it tumbled through the mist.

It clattered to the ground that seemed miles away, skidding to a stop at the edge of visibility in the swirling fog. The sound of it landing echoed strangely, as if coming from everywhere and nowhere at once.

I stood frozen, my empty hand still extended, pain throbbing through my wrist and up my arm. The monster towered over me, seeming larger than before, more substantial. The chains binding it hummed with increased intensity, but they didn't restrain it as effectively anymore. Maybe my strike had weakened them instead of the creature.

Cold realization washed over me. I was alone here, facing something ancient and evil, with an injured wrist, no weapon, and a dead colleague lying at my feet. The situation couldn't possibly get worse.

The monster moved too fast to track. A cold and impossibly strong hand clamped around my throat. My feet left the ground, dangling uselessly as it hoisted me up to its eye level. The pressure on my windpipe was immediate and absolute.

The glacial energy emanating from the monster's grip went right through my skin to my soul. My lungs seized, and the instinctive inhale I tried to take yielded nothing but a pathetic wheeze.

Panic exploded through me, firing up all of my nerve endings. My hands flew to my throat, frantically clawing at the shadowy appendage cutting off my air. But my fingers—solid, human fingers—slipped partway through the creature's hand. I could feel it there, frigid and real against my neck, but my desperate attempts to pry it loose were as effective as catching the wind.

I kicked wildly, finding nothing to connect with. I swung forward, backward, trying to build momentum to twist free, but the monster held me steady with insulting ease. Stars began to burst at the edge of my vision as my oxygen-starved brain sent up distress flares.

Somewhere distant, I heard Ghost barking frantically. My psychopomp must have sensed my peril, but she couldn't find me. Neither could Corvus. I sent a plea for help down the channel to Killion.

Only emptiness came back.

I changed tactics, forming a fist and punching the creature in the face. My hand plunged partially into its form, meeting resistance that closed around my skin. I tried to pull back, but the shadow substance clung to me, reluctant to let go.

A sick, phosphorescent light began to pulse within its amorphous body, gaining intensity with each throb. It reminded me of bioluminescent algae, but this was diseased and corrupt.

The grip on my throat remained unyielding, but now I felt something else—a sensation like ice water being injected directly into my veins, starting at my neck and spreading rapidly.

Tiny pinpricks of that same unnatural light appeared beneath the surface of the skin on my hands. They weren't stationary—they were moving, crawling under my skin like luminous ants, following the pathways of my blood vessels and spreading outward.

Parasites. The thing was infecting me.

Unable to look away, I trembled as my coloring turned an ashy gray-blue along those paths. I could feel the parasites branching across my chest, my arms, and climbing up my neck toward my face. I watched myself being consumed by some horror-movie special effect, except the pain was excruciating and unmistakably real.

Each one felt like a tiny shard of ice burrowing deeper into me, carrying a fragment of the monster's essence. My blood became sluggish. The sensation was alien and terrifying—being colonized from within by pure evil.

I tried to scream, but no sound escaped my constricted throat. The fear was overwhelming. This was primal terror, the knowledge that something was violating the most basic boundaries of self.

Everything faded, leaving only shades of gray with that sickening luminescence standing out in sharp contrast. Details blurred, the misty landscape becoming even more indistinct.

My life force drained away. Whatever these parasites were, they were feeding on my soul.

My struggles grew weaker. The frantic kicking of my legs slowed to sporadic twitches. My arms became lead weights. Even the burning in my lungs began to fade, not because I could breathe, but because my body was shutting down, one system at a time.

Distantly, I was aware that I should be fighting harder. I was Grim Zero. I had faced death before—I *worked* for Death. But none of that seemed to matter as the parasites continued their invasion, each adding to the overwhelming deep freeze seeping through me.

Chunks of hair fell out. My eyelids fluttered, so heavy now I could barely keep them open. Some detached part of my mind wondered if this was how I would end—not heroically in battle, but as a husk drained by some nameless horror.

The thought of Killion entered my fading consciousness. The image of his face, always so controlled but with eyes that revealed everything to me, surfaced. I tried to hold onto it, to draw strength from it, but even that was slipping away.

The ice reached my core, and I felt crystals forming in my heart. Each beat grew more labored than the last. I couldn't remember why I was fighting anymore, or even what fighting meant.

I was too far gone for pain. Instead, the parasites felt like they belonged there, like they were becoming part of me, or I was becoming part of them. The distinction seemed less important with each passing second.

Images flashed behind my eyes, sounds tickled my ears—my parents' soft murmurs over coffee, Ghost curled on my lap, Corvus preening his feathers, Killion's rare smile. They seemed to belong to someone else, someone I had known long ago.

The monster's grip remained unyielding, but I no longer cared. The struggle was over. The darkness at the edges of my vision consumed more and more until only a pinprick of awareness remained.

In that final moment of clarity, before everything faded completely, I saw something unexpected. Deep within the monster's churning form, past the parasites, corruption, and hungry void, there was a spark—a tiny point of light, different from the sickly shimmer of everything else. It was pure, untainted, and innocent.

A puppy. A black mastiff puppy.

My consciousness reached for it, drawn to its pure soul light in this nightmare. I saw it all then. The poor thing had been infused with the curse, the parasites taking it over, and then it had been used to deliver the curse to Silas.

As my spirit gave in, the dog's single point of light was the last thing I saw, a beacon calling to me as I slipped away into nothingness.

21

*T*hat tiny spark of light didn't go out. It grew
more distinct, even as my consciousness faded,
as if the closer I came to complete darkness, the more
clearly I could see it.

I focused on it with my last shred of awareness, and
the spark responded, brightening and taking shape. The
small, frightened mastiff puppy whined. For a moment, I
wondered if my oxygen-starved brain was hallucinating.

But this was no hallucination. The puppy existed in a
bubble of purity amidst the corruption. It wasn't only an
animal—it was the container, used to hold the curse. An
innocent life force, twisted and bound by dark magic,
forced to serve as the anchor for something monstrous.

I realized that the chains of energy binding the
monster weren't restraining it; they were anchoring the
puppy's essence to the creature, preventing it from escap-
ing. The beast wasn't the curse itself but the hideous shell
that had formed around this pure life. The curse monster

fed off it, using the puppy's vitality to fuel its unnatural existence.

The cruelty of it enraged me. The puppy looked up at me with eyes that were too sad, aware with too much understanding for a normal animal. It knew what had been done to it. It had been conscious all along, a prisoner in this corrupted form.

With everything I could still muster, I reached for its spark. I stretched my consciousness toward it, trying to offer the poor thing release, trying to break the chains that bound it to this nightmare existence.

There... The contact felt warm, grateful, and alive—so different from the parasites' icy grip. The puppy's essence reached back for me, desperate for freedom, for the peace that had been denied it.

For nothing more than a pat.

But the connection was too weak, and I was too far gone. The parasites sensed my effort and redoubled their invasion. They swarmed toward that last untainted part of my consciousness, determined to corrupt it as they had the rest of me.

Dark tendrils of their influence crossed the boundary of my awareness, dragging me back from that brief moment of connection.

My essence retreated, forced away from the puppy's light and back into my failing body. The parasites were everywhere now, claiming every cell, every atom. My connection to myself—to who and what I was—grew thinner with each passing second.

The monster had won. Sylvie was dead. I had failed.

The puppy would remain trapped, and I would become another victim of Silas Mercer's curse.

A voice cut through the darkness like a blade—familiar, commanding, and absolutely furious. At first, it was only a hiss. A gurgle. A wavering noise.

Then...

Chloe! Fight!

Killion's voice. Impossible, yet undeniable.

Fight, dragostea mea. Come back to me. The endearment carried a desperation I'd rarely heard from him. *Our souls are bound. Use it. Draw from me.*

Incatusa sufletum. Soul-bound. The magical connection that tied us together, that made us two halves of a whole.

It stirred inside me, a response so deep it bypassed conscious thought. A tiny ember that the parasites hadn't yet reached, protected by something older and stronger than the curse could ever be.

At first, it was a pinprick of heat in the center of my chest, barely noticeable against the overwhelming cold, but as Killion's voice continued to call to me, the warmth grew, spreading outward. Primal. Elemental.

Dragon energy.

The spark flared, bursting into a flame that burned hot and bright.

It raced across the barrier between worlds, feverish in my chest, spreading through my veins, following the same paths the parasites had taken but bringing purification.

Another ember ignited—my reaper power. Grim Zero magic. The two forces recognized each other, circled like dance partners, and then fused in an explosion that jolted through me, white-hot and unstoppable.

The parasites burned up. The dark veins that had spread across my skin changed from ashy gray to brilliant orange.

The monster's essence shrieked in pain as parts of itself died within me. My numb body blazed with sensation. My lungs expanded, drawing in a desperate gasp of the in-between's strange air. My heart, which had stopped, thundered like a war drum.

The magic leaped from me in a firestorm of flames that wrapped around the monster. Where my efforts to attack it had failed, this energy incinerated its defenses.

On a howl, it released its grip on my throat, more from pain than choice. I collapsed to the ground, my legs too weak to support me, but my consciousness fully returned. I watched, half in awe and half in vindictive satisfaction, as the fire spread across the cursed creature's massive form.

Its body convulsed, thrashing wildly, the purifying fire tearing through the layers of ugly evil. The sickly glow that had emanated from it died, replaced by the clean, bright light of the flames. It made a sound—not heard with ears but felt in the soul—a shriek of agony reverberating through the space.

At the center of the inferno, I watched as the chains that bound the puppy began to crack. Hairline fractures appeared, spreading outward. With each crack, the monster's form became less stable, portions of it melting and dissolving into the ether.

The shrieking intensified as the creature realized it

was dying. It tried to reform, to pull itself back together, but the fire was relentless, burning away its substance faster than it could regenerate. The chains binding the puppy shattered, shrapnel fragments of light spinning outward before fading away into nothingness.

The puppy's spirit hung suspended in the air for a moment, finally free of its prison. It glanced at me—a pure, untainted soul—and in its eyes, I saw gratitude. Then it rose upward, no longer bound to this place, and disappeared in a gentle flash of light.

The rest of the monster followed, but its end was anything but gentle. The flames consumed the last of it in a final, cataclysmic surge. Its essence disintegrated, wisps of smoke dissipating in the swirling mists.

I slumped forward. The dragon fire and reaper cocktail receded, returning to their respective sources, leaving me drained but alive. My throat ached where the monster had gripped it, and my skin tingled with the aftermath of both invasion and purification.

But the corruption was gone.

Was my magic gone, too? I'd witnessed the fire burn Andy's parasites, but also destroy his shifter magic. What had it done to mine?

Slowly, I pushed to my knees, then to my feet, swaying as I regained my balance. Sylvie's body lay nearby, a stark reminder that not everything could be undone, that some prices were permanent. After retrieving my scythe, I shuffled toward her, my steps unsteady.

"I'm sorry," I whispered, kneeling beside her. "I'll get you home." It was the least I could do.

The handle of my blade did not warm in my hand.

My tattoo did not tingle. No soul needed reaping, and yet, I feared the absence of both was due to something else.

As I gathered her broken form in my arms, I felt the connection to Killion humming in my chest—fainter now, but present. He had reached across the boundaries between worlds to pull me back from the edge. The thought comforted me as I prepared to leave this place, to return to the world of the living.

Would I be able to?

I glanced around. At least Sylvie's spirit wasn't stuck here. Not that I could see, anyway. There were no ghosts at all.

The curse was broken, the innocent puppy freed. As a reaper, I understood better than most that death was part of the natural order, but understanding didn't make it easier to bear, especially when it came for those who didn't deserve it.

I gently closed Sylvie's eyes, then stood with her in my arms, turning my back on the place where the monster had been. Digging deep, I reached out to Killion. I focused all of my awareness on our soul connection, willing any magic I still had to take me back to him.

Nothing happened.

Squeezing my eyes shut, I tightened my grip on it. "Come on," I whispered. "Killion, I need you. I need you to pull me back."

Still nothing.

My breath turned shaky as panic wormed its way into my stomach. Maybe I wasn't a grim anymore. Not a vampire.

Not anything but human.

A sob escaped my mouth. My shoulders sagged under the weight of holding Sylvie's body, understanding that I might be stuck here.

If I couldn't get back to Killion...

I'm with you. His voice made me catch my breath. *Don't give up. You. Do. Not. Give. Up.*

I hefted Sylvie's body higher and straightened my spine. Delving into the core of my being, I searched for my Grim Zero magic. Layer after layer, I dug deeper and deeper. *I know you're in there.*

The essence sat black and barren. A void.

I envisioned the cosmos, remembering the feeling of flying through universes, sharing stardust with Killion.

My mate.

You. Do. Not. Give. Up.

I chanted it in my head. *I do not give up. I do not give up. I do not give up.*

Time to use a different kind of necromancy. I poked and prodded the seemingly dead essence. Pulling more dragon fire through the channel with Killion, I directed the flames to it.

Wake up, I told it. *You're Grim Zero. You are eternal.*

Smoke rose in tendrils. The void coughed.

Like a hose, I poured more dragon fire into it, not to burn but to warm, to comfort.

To rouse.

The darkness faded. An ember sparked.

I blew on that ember, encouraging it to grow.

My spirit flickered, my blood ran hot. Sweat beaded on my forehead in contrast to the chill of the air around me.

We do not give up, I told that essence.

A chant. A mantra. A promise.

And then...

Grim Zero roared to life, enraged and tempestuous. She devoured my spirit and spit it out, knowing she could not cleave herself from me. We were one and the same.

But oh, she was furious. Ranting in my head, ready to fight me and everyone else that existed. That's when I realized that she'd finally met the one thing that could destroy her—Killion's dragon. A being from another world, another dimension. Not meant for this one like she was.

It scared her. Terrified her.

Up until now, she'd felt invincible. Even if Soul Management Group got to decide when and in what form she was incarnated, she'd always known they couldn't wipe her out. Couldn't annihilate her.

But the dragon fire had.

Almost.

How much more before she'd been exterminated with the parasites?

At the moment, it didn't matter. I allowed her lashing for a full minute so she could work through her anger, then I shoved her away. We were one, yet it often felt like this—fighting as two separate entities. Every time I thought we'd finally become fully integrated, something would happen, and we'd be back to being distinct individuals.

And not typically on the friendliest of terms.

Enough, I told her. *We need to get back to the dimension of the living. Help me.*

She swiped at me with razor-sharp claws. They missed, however, like a cat giving me a warning.

We can't stay here. This is some pocket of the in-between. It's not safe for us.

She snarled. A petulant child.

I realize you no longer feel safe with me, but the truth is, the dragon fire saved us. Both of us. Now, we use it to return home.

A tug on the bond let me know Killion was listening. He understood what I was trying to do, but he also wanted me back.

Our mate is waiting, I said to her.

Your mate, not mine, she replied.

She'd been soulmates with Death. The link between them would never be severed.

Another reason Grim Zero felt like a separate entity to me. Her bond with Death was as eternal as mine was with Killion.

What would Death want you to do? Stay here in the in-between or return to the mortal world and go back to work?

Silence. She didn't like my reasoning, but couldn't deny that she knew the truth.

The claws she'd swiped at me sank into my connection to Killion. The instant she grasped it, Killion tugged.

And I left the hazy, cold world between reality and the afterlife behind.

22

The weight of Sylvie's body in my arms was too limp, too final, as I emerged into the church.

Killion rushed to me, his face filled with worry and relief. "You're all right." He stroked my back. "I couldn't come after you without Ghost to carry me there." His gaze dropped to Sylvie. "What happened?"

I moved through the dim light of the nave, dust motes dancing in the colored beams from the stained glass windows, to gently lay her on a wooden pew that creaked beneath her slight frame. Death wasn't supposed to feel this personal, not to someone who ferried souls for a living, but somehow, it always did.

"We both died." I arranged her small hands over her chest, a mockery of peace. Her sundress was now torn and stained dark at the edges. The clogs she'd worn were gone, lost somewhere in the chaos. Without them, her feet looked impossibly small. "I came back. Sylvie didn't." I whispered, using her nickname, "Vi, I'm so sorry."

The church seemed to absorb my words, swallowing

them into the ancient stone walls that had heard countless prayers and lamentations over the centuries. St. Anne looked on, unmoved. The beams overhead were dark with age, supporting the ceiling that soared away into shadows and made me feel as small as Sylvie looked.

A warmth at my back, then Killion's arms wrapped around my waist. I leaned into him, my body recognizing safety even as my mind spun with horror and regret.

The others watched in silence.

"What happened?" Aurora asked, echoing Killion.

"I got her killed." I closed my eyes, feeling tears press against my lids. "We were sucked into the in-between by the monster connected to Silas, and I couldn't save her."

Killion's voice was firm but gentle. "This isn't your fault."

I turned in his arms, pressing my face against his chest. For a moment, I let myself be held, drawing strength from his stillness.

Katarina stood near the door, her multiple piercings catching the lights, arms crossed, and expression unreadable behind thick black eyeliner. Silas sat alone in a far corner, the dead mastiff's body stretched across the floor before him. His shoulders shook with sobs, his lanky frame bent nearly double with grief. The sight of him— this man who had caused so much trouble—brought a tangle of emotions I couldn't sort through.

"There was a puppy," I said, pulling my gaze away from him. "The mastiff. Its life force was trapped inside the monster, powering it. It had been injected with parasites."

"As in the curse?" Aurora said with a tinge of uncertainty.

I nodded. "I—*we*"—I gave Killion a pointed look— "destroyed them."

Killion stroked my back. "All of them?"

The giant mastiff's body drew my gaze once more. "Yes. The puppy was relieved to be free from the chains of the curse," I told Silas. "If that's any comfort. It went on to the afterlife."

He didn't reply, only stroked the dog's head.

"Those awful things would have drained me completely if—" I paused.

"If what?" Katarina asked sharply from her post.

"If I hadn't connected to Killion's dragon energy." I wanted to burrow into him and stay there. "I used it to burn them to ash." I rubbed a hand over my chest, feeling Grim Zero waiting, listening. *And so much more.*

I didn't mention how it had felt—like fire rushing through my veins, like being filled with ancient starlight. How for a moment, I'd understood what it meant to be something more than human, something that had existed for centuries and would continue for centuries more. Not Grim Zero's power, but something beyond this world.

"You wielded fire," Andy said with a touch of awe.

I stared at Sylvie's body. "But the monster had already..."

A particularly loud sob drew our attention to Silas, his fingers trembling against the dog's fur. "I didn't know," he whispered to the dog. "I'm so sorry, old friend."

When he looked up and caught me watching, his red-rimmed eyes shifted to Sylvie. Guilt flashed across his face before he quickly looked away.

"Silas didn't make the monster," I said to the others. "I don't think he knew what it was capable of."

"Perhaps not," Killion replied, his voice equally low. "But he fueled it and commanded it. That makes him culpable nonetheless."

Responsibility was something I understood all too well. "I have to alert SMG and Death."

Killion's hand found mine, his fingers cool against my skin. "There could be consequences. You're the only witness to what happened."

Andy and Aurora both frowned. Above us, the ancient beams seemed to groan slightly, as if the church itself was weighing the burden of what had occurred beyond its walls. Through my disquiet, I understood what he was suggesting, even though it was hard to accept. "They might think I did it."

Killion nodded. "They have insisted there was no curse, and Sylvie was investigating you."

I looked down at my hands, remembering how the parasites had felt as they tried to bore into my power. They had been hungry, desperate things—not so different from people, in the end. We all want something. We all reach for it, sometimes destroying ourselves and others in the process.

My heart beat in my throat. "I could have saved her."

Killion's fingers tightened around mine. "You don't know that."

"I do. If I'd recognized what the monster was faster, if I'd connected to your power sooner—"

"Chloe." He forced me to look at him, his violet eyes holding mine. "This path leads nowhere. Trust me. I have walked it for centuries."

The church fell quiet except for Silas's diminishing sobs. On the pew, Sylvie remained motionless, beyond all care of changing light or heavy conversations.

"Soul Management Group will want answers," I said finally.

"We should go over your statement," Killion replied. "While you have nothing to hide, it will be important to make them understand they were wrong about the curse."

"Andy and I will vouch for you," Aurora said, standing. "We all saw the damage the parasites did."

Andy raised a weary hand. "My testimony about the invasion should carry all the weight you need."

I nodded, though a nagging sensation told me the truth might not be enough—not with the complicated politics of the supernatural world, and not with the rules I'd bent and broken in my attempts to help others.

"Even if you convince them you didn't kill her, they can claim you put her in danger," Killion said, pacing. "At best, they'll revoke your reaper status."

"But I'm still Grim Zero," I said, though uncertainty crept into my tone. "They can't take that from me."

"Mei has been upset with your methods since the beginning," he replied. "You've defied her repeatedly. This could give her the leverage she needs to put Grim Zero on ice permanently."

My stomach dropped. I opened my mouth to respond when a sudden draft swept through the church. The heavy wooden doors at the entrance groaned, their ancient hinges protesting as they swung wide. Everyone tensed, and Katarina crouched, ready to attack.

Harlow entered, a grin on her face. But it was the three figures that followed her that made all of us relax.

The vampire family we'd been searching for—Cormac, Roma, and Rena—moved hesitantly into the nave. Cormac, tall and broad-shouldered with chestnut hair, had a supportive arm wrapped protectively around his wife. Roma's dark hair was matted, her appearance disheveled. Clasping her hand was their daughter. Her eyes were wide, darting around the church as if expecting an attack from the shadows.

"You rescued them," I breathed.

Harlow nodded. "They were in the old factory district. The cords to Silas were gone, and they were easily revived."

The family looked relatively unharmed, though their clothes were dirty and torn. Roma had scratches along her arms—not deep enough to threaten a vampire, but evidence of rough treatment. The little girl clutched a tattered stuffed rabbit, her knuckles white around its worn fabric.

"Are you okay?" I asked them.

"Disoriented," Harlow answered for them. "They were kept in magically induced stasis. It'll take time for them to recover fully."

From his place in the corner, Silas rose to his feet. The vampires tensed. With trembling hands, he removed his worn hat, clutching it against his chest as he took a few halting steps forward.

In a blur of movement, Killion positioned himself between Silas and the family. "That's close enough," he warned.

"Please," Silas said. His voice was rough from crying over his dog. "I need to speak to them."

Cormac's face hardened. "You did this to us."

Silas nodded, his lanky frame seeming to shrink further. "I did." His eyes flicked to the dead mastiff, then to Sylvie's body, before returning to the vampire family. "And I can't undo it. Any of it. But I need you to know it wasn't supposed to turn out like this."

Roma's laugh was brittle. "You were planning to kill us."

"No. That was never my plan." He took another step forward, stopping when Killion's growl rumbled through the church. Rena shifted behind her father's legs. "I work for Soul Management Group, just like her." He pointed at me. "They've used me for wrongdoing, and I needed help to break a curse so I could get away from them. I knew kidnapping you would give me leverage with Chloe and Killion. You were a means to an end."

"All the more reason I should kill you," Cormac said, flashing his fangs. "You're lucky we follow Killion's codes."

The little girl peered around her father's leg, her eyes, far older than her age, studied Silas with eerie intensity. "You hurt Bunny," she said, squeezing her stuffed rabbit with its torn ear.

Something in Silas seemed to break at her words. His shoulders sagged further, and when he spoke again, his voice cracked. "I'm sorry, little one. My life is worthless and I take responsibility for the pain I've inflicted, but…"

"He *was* cursed," I told Cormac and Roma. "I'm not justifying what he did, but he lost his family to rogue vampires, and SMG forced him into a life of wiping out factions they considered liabilities."

"It's true," Killion said. "But the curse is now broken. Mercer is free of it and what it forced him to do. There are consequences he must face, but the first is asking your forgiveness."

"You caged my family," Roma snarled at the former hunter. "My daughter. We were conscious the entire time, did you know that? The stasis prevented movement, not awareness. We felt everything you did to us. Felt those horrible…creatures invading us."

Silas flinched. "I didn't know about the parasites. They were part of the curse. I know it doesn't change what happened, but I am sorry, truly. The curse left me with little control."

Rena tugged on her mother's hand, drawing her attention down. They exchanged a look—one of those silent communications that families develop—before Roma sighed and returned her gaze to Silas.

"Rena claims your grief is real." She nodded toward her daughter. "She has always been sensitive to emotions. But understanding does not equal forgiveness."

"I don't expect you to forgive me," he replied. "I don't deserve it. I just… I needed you to know the truth."

Rena, still clutching her rabbit, stepped away from her parents and approached Silas. Both Cormac and

Roma tensed but didn't stop her. Killion watched with predator-sharp focus, ready to move if needed.

The child stopped a few feet from the man, her head tilted up as she studied him. "Your dog forgives you," she said simply. "He says you didn't know."

Silas's breath caught. He kneeled to look her in the eyes. "You can...talk to him?"

Rena nodded solemnly. "He's confused, but not angry." She glanced toward the mastiff's body. "He says to remember the creek with the flat stones. Whatever that means."

Tears spilled down Silas's weather-worn cheeks, but he managed a shaky smile. "It was our favorite place to go. He would run for hours on the banks and swim in the water." His voice hitched. "Thank you," he whispered. "Thank you for telling me that."

The simple exchange—painful, honest, unexpected —seemed to release the tension in the church. Not forgiveness, perhaps, but recognition of shared grief and pain. It was, I thought, about as much resolution as anyone could hope for in the aftermath of something so terrible.

In the midst of this disaster, we had at least managed to achieve this small victory. The family was safe. The monster was defeated. The suffering puppy was in a much better place.

The air near the altar shimmered and folded in on itself. Mei Han appeared as a wispy holograph. Her crisp black suit looked impossibly out of place—a slice of corporate efficiency inserted into our messy group.

Killion's hand caught mine, and I felt the coiled readiness in his posture. The vampire family drew closer together. Even Silas straightened, brushing tears from his face as he watched Mei take all of us. Her focus narrowed on Sylvie for a long, pregnant moment.

Her hair was pulled back so tightly it seemed to stretch her features. Only her eyes moved freely, locking onto me. "Grim 281," she said, her voice carrying the emotionless clarity of a bell tolling midnight. "You are hereby suspended from all reaper duties, effective immediately."

The words hit like physical blows. Grim Zero hissed and turned her claws toward her. Grim 281 was my current designation, and even though Mei knew I was the original reaper, she used it to humble me. Remind me to stay in line. "On what grounds?" I fired at her. "Sylvie's death is not my fault." *At least, not technically.* I couldn't have known either of us would be yanked into the in-between, especially not her. Couldn't know the monster would kill her.

Mei's lips thinned. "Reckless endangerment of Soul Management Group assets. Refusing to carry out your assigned duties. Bending and breaking every rule in the SMG Code of Conduct book. And now, the death of an Internal Affairs agent."

"I haven't even come close to breaking every rule in the code book," I argued. True, but small comfort at the moment. "And I'll say it again—Silas had a curse placed on him by one of you at SMG, and it created a parasitic monster that was about to destroy innocent animals, as well as supernaturals in my town. I broke the curse. You can thank me anytime."

"Save your speech for the board," she snapped. "You will present yourself at headquarters in twenty-four hours for a formal review. Your credentials are suspended until further notice."

A cold, hard lump settled in my stomach. A dozen arguments ran through my head. Grim Zero scratched against the container that held her, wanting to get to Mei. To lay her low.

"This is unjust," Killion said. "Chloe has uncovered a plot inside your walls and stopped a supernatural threat to all of us."

Mei didn't waver. "Rules exist for a reason, vampire. Your attachment to Grim 281 has clearly clouded your judgment."

"It's Grim Zero," I said, my voice rising. The temperature dropped so rapidly that I could see my breath cloud in front of me. Candles that had been guttering on the altar flared bright, then died completely. The shadows in the corners seemed to deepen, to move with purpose.

"Reaper's keepers," I whispered, recognizing the signs. "Here comes Death."

23

A column of darkness materialized beside one of the stone pillars.

Death surveyed the room with casual interest. Muscles bulged beneath a khaki colored shirt and green vest with multiple pockets, and his cargo pants ended in scuffed boots. "G'day, mates," he said, affecting his stupid Australian accent. He looked as out of place as Mei did. "Hope I'm not interrupting something important."

He'd made himself visible to everyone. Mei's posture turned to steel. The vampires, outside of Killion, took subtle steps back. Silas looked as though he might faint, his already pale face going ashen.

"Death," Mei said, her voice tight and annoyed. "We weren't expecting you."

"Well, that's the fun part about being me, isn't it?" he replied, leaping off the dais, the impact of his landing resounding in the air. "Never expected, always arriving." He winked at me.

I had no clue why.

"Why are you here?" Mei asked.

Death pointed at Sylvie's body. "A bit obvious, isn't it? Your Internal Affairs agent is dead, and it sounds as if you're accusing my grim of lying about what happened." He moved toward the pew, examining Sylvie with clinical detachment. "Nasty business, this. Magical construct with parasitic capabilities." He glanced over to Silas. "Someone's been playing with very old, very forbidden magic."

Silas seemed to shrink further under Death's scrutiny. "It wasn't me playing with that magic. It was them." He pointed in the general direction of Mei's holograph. "One of them cursed me and forced me to hunt supernaturals they wanted out of the picture."

"The situation is under control," Mei insisted. "Grim 281 has been suspended pending review. The responsible party—" she nodded toward Silas "—will be taken into custody for processing."

"I'm the victim here," Silas argued. "You and your cronies did this to me. You even sent that poor dog"—he pointed at the mastiff—"to me to keep me under control. I had no idea."

"Mmm." Death circled around to stand next to me. "And what about our dead agent?"

"Her family will be notified. Her service record will reflect her sacrifice," Mei replied.

Death's smile was sharp enough to cut stone. "Her service record? That's all you're concerned about?" He shook his head. "Sylvie Pearson was nothing but a gopher before you installed her as an IA agent. More importantly, she was in the middle of several critical investigations when she died. Isn't that right?"

"Investigations that now cannot be completed," Mei stated flatly, "thanks to your grim."

Killion stiffened, and he flooded our telepathic channel with theories of why *Mei* might want Sylvie out of the picture.

Wait...had that been the plan all along? To send Sylvie to her death, or at least sidetrack her other investigations?

"Unless..." Death flicked his attention to me, his eyes glittering with something that might have been mischief or malice—with him, it was hard to tell. All I knew for certain was that he was up to something. "Unless Chloe here gives us a hand."

"What?" Mei's voice held a note of confusion. Had to admit, I was right there with her.

Death flipped his hand between me and Sylvie. "Chloe, raise Agent Pearson for me. I need to ask her a few questions about what she was looking into. And then"—he snapped his fingers—"we can get her statement on what happened with you and that monster. Win-win."

The church went utterly silent. Even the dust motes seemed to freeze. Raising the dead—true necromancy was one of the most strictly regulated abilities in the Code of Conduct manual. It was also one of my talents that Soul Management Group preferred I keep under wraps.

Mei waved both hands. "Absolutely not. Grim 281 is suspended. She is not authorized to perform any supernatural activities, especially not necromancy."

"It's Grim Zero," I snapped.

Death raised a brow—not at me, at her. "Don't you want the truth, Mei? Or are you hiding something?"

"Protocol is clear," she insisted. "An agent under suspension cannot—"

"I don't give a rat's arse about protocol," he interrupted. "What I care about is finding out what happened to Sylvie and why you picked her to be your lone investigator for Internal Affairs. Silas Mercer is right—something's rotten in Soul Management Group. I intend to find out what. Or who."

The implications of his statement hung like a lightning strike between all of us. Death wasn't only agreeing with me that there was corruption within the organization; he was also challenging Mei to prove that she wasn't behind it.

Mei's expression turned her face into a mask of controlled fury. "Grim 281, I am giving you a direct order. Do not attempt to raise Agent Pearson. If you defy this order, I will ensure your permanent removal from Soul Management Group and the revocation of all supernatural privileges."

Death countered immediately. "And I'm giving you a different order. Raise her, *Grim Zero*. I need to know what she discovered."

Being caught between Death and Soul Management's bureaucracy was like being trapped between a hurricane and an avalanche—no good options, just different ways to be destroyed. I glanced at Killion, but his face was carefully neutral. This was my decision to make.

"Chloe," Mei's voice was ice, but I didn't miss her switch to using my name. "Consider your future carefully."

"I'd offer the same advice to you, Mei," Death said. "Refusing my request suggests you're involved in this shady, dark magic."

"That's preposterous," she said.

Stepping away from Killion, I moved to Sylvie's body, feeling everyone's eyes on me. The weight of their attention was a physical pressure on my skin.

"I'm sorry," I whispered to Sylvie.

"Grim 281, don't you dare—" Mei began.

I knelt beside the pew, blocking out her voice and everything else except the still form before me. Sylvie looked peaceful—more peaceful than she'd had any right to be, considering how she died. I placed a hand gently over her heart, feeling the unnatural cold of her body through the fabric of her dress.

Necromancy for me wasn't like in the movies. No dramatic incantations, no swirling mist or supernatural light. Grim Zero sighed as if sinking into a warm bathtub, the desire to give life as natural as breathing. For us, reviving the dead was a quiet and intimate experience. A conversation between one who walked between worlds and one who had crossed over. I closed my eyes, reaching for that part of myself that could see beyond the veil, and pushed deeper, to the part that could pull back what had passed through.

The church grew distant. My body felt lighter. I was in

no way ready to head into the in-between, but I didn't have to. All I needed to do was pull her through.

Beneath my palms, I felt a subtle vibration, like the memory of a heartbeat. "Vi," I whispered, using her nickname. "I need you to come back."

Power flowed from me into her, a sensation like water running through my veins, draining downward. My energy, my essence, flowing into the empty vessel that had been Sylvie Pearson.

I was vaguely aware of Mei shouting something, of Killion moving closer to protect me, of Death's satisfied smile. But my focus remained on the body beneath my hands and the tenuous connection I was building to the soul that had departed it. Her face flashed through my mind. Her smile. Her confidence.

There you are. I could feel her soul responding to my call, reluctant but unable to resist the pull of necromantic energy. A flutter, like a bird's wing beating against glass. Then another. Sylvie's chest rose ever so slightly, then fell. Rose again.

Her eyelids twitched.

I poured more into the connection, feeling light-headed as my energy drained faster. Grim Zero smiled, wicked and happy to defy Mei. It had always been easy for me to raise animals. I did that with barely a thought. Humans were different.

"That's enough, Chloe," Death said quietly from behind me. "She's coming."

A gasp tore through the church as Sylvie's eyes flew open, her back arching off the pew in a sudden, violent inhale. Her gaze was unfocused, confused, the eyes of someone ripped from one reality and thrust into another without warning or consent.

"What—?" she heaved, her voice raspy. "What's happening?"

"You were dead," I said, hating to break the news to her without any warmup. "But we need to talk."

24

$\mathcal{I}$ helped Sylvie sit up on the hard wooden pew, her fingers going to her neck, her eyes still glazed with the memory of death. Her breathing came in irregular bursts, her movements jerky, because her soul hadn't fully settled back into their body.

"Take your time," I said. "There's no rush."

But there was. I could feel Mei's holographic presence at the edge of our circle. Her projection flickered occasionally, betraying either a technical glitch or her impatience—I suspected the latter.

Killion stood behind me, a silent sentinel. Silas, Andy, and Aurora moved closer as Death made himself comfortable next to Sylvie. Not crowding her, but intimidating all the same.

The Aldrichs left with Harlow to go home. They planned to stop by the penthouse to pick up Redemption on the way. Katarina had disappeared, as well. No telling where she'd gone.

Sylvie swallowed hard, the sound audible in the

hushed space. "I—" she started, then stopped, pressing her palm flat against her sternum as though checking that her heart was beating. "I was dead?"

"Yes," I confirmed, not seeing any point in sugarcoating it. "I resurrected you. Under Death's orders."

Her eyes looked hollow as they met mine and avoided my boss's. "Why?"

"So you can validate Chloe's story about your demise," Death answered. "You were sucked into the in-between with her and something killed you. What do you remember?"

"I..." She paused, her forehead creasing. Her hand rubbed at her throat again. There was a raw, ragged bruise there. "It happened so fast," she continued. "I was talking to Chloe. I didn't understand where I was." A visible shudder ran through her body. "There was this... mass. It grabbed me and started choking me. It was so strong." Her voice hiccupped.

I laid a hand on her arm, acutely aware of Mei's intense attention. She still didn't believe me about the curse that had created a monster. Maybe now she would.

"I tried to call out," Sylvie continued, "but its hands were around my throat." Her fingers touched her neck again, tracing the memory of violence. "It was cold. So cold it burned. And then—" She closed her eyes briefly. "I heard my neck snap. I felt it."

Silas exhaled. Killion shifted. Aurora gripped Andy's hand.

The sound still echoed in my memory. "Do you recall anything after that?" I prompted.

Sylvie's expression took on a faraway look. "I was

floating. Above my body. I saw you." Her gaze shifted to me, filled with something like wonder. "It killed you, too, didn't it? But then you were glowing, burning. The thing recoiled, and…" She blinked. "Did you destroy it?"

"I did."

"Anything else?" Death asked.

"I was pulled somewhere else. Not here, not…any-where I recognized. It was dark, but not completely. Like twilight underwater." She frowned, clearly struggling to articulate the experience. "I couldn't move forward or back. And I wasn't alone."

My skin prickled at those words. The in-between, the threshold space where souls waited before moving on, was not a place the living were meant to know about.

"What did you see there?" Mei's voice cut through the tension, clinical and detached.

Sylvie looked up at the hologram, her expression hardening. "Not much. It was too dark. But I felt things moving past me. Other souls, maybe?"

"Most likely," I said.

"Then I was yanked back. Hard. Like being pulled through a keyhole too small for my body. And here I am." Her hands balled into fists in her lap, knuckles white. "That thing wasn't a ghost. It wasn't a poltergeist. It was something else entirely." She looked around at all of us, her gaze finally settling on Mei. "It was real," she insisted, her voice cracking slightly. "The monster exists. Or did. I felt it kill me."

The words hung in the air like a verdict.

"I'm so sorry," Silas said. "I had no idea the curse had a physical manifestation that could…kill."

"It's gone," I said, straightening despite my body's protests. "Both the monster and the curse that created it. The container for the curse was the mastiff, only in puppy form," I told Sylvie before I glanced meaningfully at Silas. "When I destroyed the monster, its spirit was freed."

Sylvie stared at me, her expression a mixture of awe and something more complicated—perhaps the peculiar intimacy that comes from having someone literally save your soul. "Thank you," she said simply.

I waved away her gratitude. "You can thank me by helping ensure SMG takes this seriously." I turned to Mei. "I released the dog from the curse's bonds and broke the curse itself, but we still don't know who put the curse on Silas to begin with, or who manipulated him into working as a supernatural hunter. Any ideas?"

The accusation in my tone couldn't be missed.

"This is...concerning information," she said finally, her voice measured. "Of course, Soul Management Group takes any threat to supernatural order seriously. I'll need to verify the details of what's occurred before proceeding."

Irritation burned in my veins, akin to the dragon fire. Even with a firsthand account from an SMG employee who had literally died, she was still hedging. "Verify?" I repeated, not bothering to keep the incredulousness from my voice. "Sylvie just gave you her account of being killed by this thing and seeing me destroy it. What exactly needs verification?"

The hologram flickered. "Protocol requires thorough documentation of all supernatural incidents. You know that. Especially those involving fatalities and resurrections." Her eyes shifted to the left—a classic tell for deception. Her fingers tapped against her thigh in a rapid pattern that belied her calm tone. And most damning of all, the slight upward tilt of her chin as she finished with, "I'll initiate an investigation immediately upon my return to headquarters."

"You have no intention of investigating this," I said flatly.

She glared at me. "That's a serious accusation, Grim 281."

I swore under my breath. She wouldn't ever call me by my proper designation.

I stepped closer to her projection, noting how she instinctively leaned away despite not being physically present. "Your body language gives you away. You're already categorizing this as a non-event, aren't you?"

A flicker of something—annoyance? fear?—crossed her features before the professional mask slipped back into place. "I understand you've been through a traumatic experience."

"Don't patronize me." I earned a warning look from Killion that I promptly ignored. "Sylvie died. I fought a literal manifestation of cursed energy. These are facts, not trauma-induced delusions."

Mei spread her hands in a placating gesture that made my teeth clench. "Of course, *Grim Zero*. And all facts will be given due consideration in the official report."

Her use of my correct title was flippant, not respectful. "Which will be filed where, exactly?" I pressed.

"When will the board meet to discuss this? I'd like to be present."

Sylvie looked between Mei and me, her expression troubled. "Me, too," she said.

"I assure you, I will personally oversee this investigation." Mei's voice was smooth as polished marble and just as cold. "SMG values the safety of all supernatural entities under its jurisdiction. I'll let you know if you're presence is requested."

The rehearsed quality of her words made me laugh. Corporate platitudes designed to pacify while promising nothing. I'd heard similar phrases in her responses to some of my previous reports, right before they disappeared into administrative oblivion.

Sylvie struggled to her feet, steadying herself against the pew. "Ms. Han," she said, her voice stronger than I expected, "I reviewed most of Chloe's cases before I inserted myself into her life. She has a track record of being correct about many of the things listed in them that SMG didn't investigate. She was right this time about the curse. Maybe you should actually listen to her more often."

Mei went ramrod straight. "Your input is noted. Your experience with this will certainly factor into our assessment."

Meaning it would be filed away and forgotten, just like everything else.

The distant sound of traffic and the occasional creak of the old building filled the air. The tension hung heavy, pressing against my already aching body. Silas pulled a silver flask from inside his duster and took a quick swig before offering it to Sylvie, who hesitated only momentarily before accepting.

"Well," I said finally, meeting the eyes of everyone in the room. "We'll eagerly await the results of that investigation, won't we?"

Death crossed his arms over his massive chest. Killion stood glaring at her. Silas and Sylvie stood immobile on one side of us, Andy and Aurora on the other.

Mei's hologram gave a tight smile. "Indeed. I should return to headquarters to begin the process. And Sylvie must return to the other side."

"Sylvie Pearson's soul contract isn't up," Death said without preamble. "I am officially reinstating her."

If I hadn't been watching Mei, I might have missed the flicker of genuine alarm that crossed her face before she composed herself. "You can't do that," she said.

Even as a hologram, squaring off against Death required either immense courage or profound stupidity. I wasn't sure which Mei possessed in greater quantity. Death's smile was all teeth. "Can't I?" He cocked his head, regarding her with the casual interest of a predator deciding whether a potential meal was worth the effort of chasing. "Funny thing about being Death—it tends to give one certain privileges when it comes to soul contracts."

"There are protocols," she insisted, though her voice had lost some of its confidence. "The Soul Management Group board must approve any contract reinstatements, especially for SMG employees. You know the rules."

"Rules." Death repeated the word like he was tasting it. "Yes, let's talk about rules, shall we? Like the rule that says SMG executives cannot withhold information about supernatural threats from field agents. Or the rule prohibiting the board from ignoring credible reports about conflict of interest when assigning cases." His gaze slid briefly to me, and I felt a chill that had nothing to do with a drop in temperature. "Or perhaps the most important rule—that SMG exists to manage souls, not exploit them."

Mei's voice was brittle. "Subtle accusations they may be, but they are completely unfounded."

"Are they?" Death shrugged. "Because Sylvie has found quite a bit of foundation for them, haven't you, luv?"

All eyes turned to her. She straightened despite her obvious exhaustion. "I was recruited specifically by Death," she said, her voice steady, "to investigate board misconduct, especially in light of Silas Mercer's claims."

I felt as though someone had pulled the floor out from under me. Sylvie was an undercover agent for *Death*?

Now, I understood the wink.

He'd been up to this all along.

My gaze flew to Killion, whose raised eyebrows indicated he was as surprised as I was. Only Silas seemed less shocked, his expression calculating as he studied her with newfound respect.

"I promoted you to Internal Affairs," Mei said. "Your job was to investigate field agents, not the board."

"A convenient cover," Death interjected. "Who better to move freely through SMG operations than someone checking credentials and protocols? No department closes its doors to Internal Affairs. That's why I suggested it when you continually voiced concerns about Chloe's actions."

I gawked. "You did *what*?"

Sylvie met my eyes. "Your behavior pattern flagged as potentially risky—breaking protocols, going off-book on assignments. When you refused to harvest Silas and made the claim about the curse, Death decided to have me look into it."

I glared at my boss, even though I silently high-fived him. "That's why you were talking to Sylvie in the parking lot that day." It all fell into place. "You believed me all along."

He chuffed and waved it off. "I wanted to know if you were part of the problem. As you so often are."

Sylvie offered a small, apologetic smile. "It didn't take long to realize you were just stubborn, not corrupt."

"Thanks. I think," I muttered.

Death's laughter filled the church, a sound like distant thunder. "Chloe Frost, corrupt? That would be like suspecting a Labrador of plotting world domination." He cocked a thumb in my direction. "Earnest to a fault, this one."

I scowled at him while Mei's hologram solidified as she seemed to gather herself. "This is outrageous. Secret investigations, accusations without formal review, reinstatement of contracts without authorization—the board will not stand for this breach of protocol."

"The board," Death said, all traces of humor vanishing from his eyes, and his accent fading with it, "will be too busy defending itself against formal charges to stand for much of anything. I am filing a petition with SMG's oversight committee for a full investigation into the board's activities, with special attention to the unauthorized collection of soul energy and the creation of cursed artifacts."

Silas drew closer. "You have proof? Actual, documented proof?"

"We do now," Death nodded toward Sylvie. "Sylvie's death at the hands of the monster—one created using magic that only the highest-ranking SMG employees have access to—provides the final link we need."

Mei blinked. "You've been planning this."

"For longer than I'd like," Death confirmed. "Some of us take the natural order seriously, Mei. Universal balance can never be achieved if you're rigging things from the other side."

"You knew," I said, still processing it as I turned to him. "You knew I was right about the curse and all that other stuff. This whole time, you knew, and you let me think I was crazy and paranoid."

Death had the grace to look slightly abashed, though on his imposing frame, the expression seemed out of place. "I needed more than theories. I needed irrefutable proof that would stand up to an oversight committee. And I knew between you and Sylvie, you'd get that proof for me."

A complex set of emotions wound through me—anger at being kept in the dark, vindication that my suspicions had been correct all along, and an uncomfortable warmth at Death's apparent confidence in my abilities. "You should have told me."

"Perhaps," he acknowledged. "But would you have acted naturally if you'd known? Would Mei and the others have suspected a trap if you'd been aware of it?"

He had a point.

"This is all very dramatic," Mei said, "but you're overlooking one crucial detail. The oversight committee reports to the board. Your petition will go nowhere."

Death's smile returned, cold and brutal. "Under normal circumstances, yes. But when the petition comes with evidence of direct endangerment to the veil between life and death? Even your handpicked committee members won't be able to bury that. The cosmic implications alone will force their hands."

I saw the moment when calculation replaced shock. Mei was already planning her counterattack. Already figuring out how to spin this, how to minimize the damage. "This isn't over," she said, her voice clipped.

Death smiled. "On that," he said, "we are in complete agreement."

The hologram flickered once, then vanished, leaving the church feeling somehow larger and emptier.

Ghost emerged from under a pew, trotting to my side and nudging me with her nose. Katarina strode down the aisle, giving me a quick nod to let me know she'd brought my dog just in case I needed her.

"So," I said, breaking the loaded silence, "anyone want to tell me exactly how much of the last year of my life has been an elaborate sting operation?"

Death's laughter was genuine. "Not all of it, reaper. Just the interesting bits."

That wasn't particularly comforting.

25

*S*ylvie straightened her sundress, smoothed her hair, and then looked directly at where Mei Han's hologram had been. She was no longer showing any sign of the jerky, mechanical movements from before.

"I need to think about whether I'm going back to SMG," she announced, flicking a quick gaze to Death. "I believed in what we were doing—protecting the balance between life and death, maintaining the natural order. But now?" She shook her head, her expression troubled. "I question everything about the organization. *Everything.*"

Silas nodded. "You should."

Death regarded Sylvie with approval. "Questioning is the beginning of wisdom," he said, sounding uncharacteristically philosophical. "And we could use wisdom in the days ahead."

Ghost pressed against my leg, her warm, solid presence a reminder that some things remained constant even when everything else changed. I picked her up and hugged her to me.

SEVERAL EVENTS OCCURRED in quick succession over the next few days: Silas and Sylvie gave full testimonies to the board, clearing me of all wrongdoing; Death informed me that Mei was under investigation; and Sylvie officially quit her job.

With Soul Management Group, at least. Her job with me was still available, and I was ever so grateful for her help getting the clinic back to normal.

The parasites were gone, and our clinic was back to its usual chaos. Silas hung around up front, keeping her company. He had no job and no dog, so he moped, seemingly lost, but Sylvie was good for him, and she managed to get some work out of him as the week wore on. He took over janitorial duties just to be close to her.

The place had never been cleaner or more organized. All the animals affected by the parasites had been given a clean bill of health. That Thursday, my colleagues and I performed three morning surgeries, two dental procedures, and met for an office update over lunch.

Sylvie had contacted an anesthesiologist who was willing to work part-time. The gal couldn't start right away, but we could muddle through a few more weeks before she moved to town. Nita was nearly done with her classes and would take her boards in June. By summer, we'd have things more under control.

I hoped.

The front bell jingled as Dr. O'Leary, JR, and I were

finishing our meeting. The relief on their faces, knowing that we were expanding our staff, was a welcome sight.

Sylvie called out, "The puppies are here!"

I swallowed my last bite of sandwich and ran to the front. "Hey," I said to Miss Vera, my former landlady, and her sister, Miss Velma. "Thanks for coming."

"The puppies are doing great," Velma said. She was dressed in jeans and a bright green tunic. "Why do you need to see them again already?"

Vera hugged me, nearly matching her sister in blue khakis and a similar bright green shirt. "You look like you haven't slept in ages. And you're so thin! I'm going to bring you some food."

That was Vera, always mothering me. "It's been a rough week," I admitted. "I need the puppies for him." I pointed to Silas.

His face lit up with surprise. He no longer dressed like an old cowboy. Sylvie had redone his wardrobe, and today he wore a polo shirt and a pair of faded jeans. "Me?"

Sylvie opened the carrier doors, and five puppies spilled out in an assortment of shades of brown and black. "They're adorable!"

"They're a mastiff mix," I said. "All looking for a good home."

He tensed, his eyes meeting mine. "Oh, I don't know..."

I patted his shoulder. "It may feel too soon, but animals have this innate way of healing even the deepest wounds."

"Silas, look at this one." Sylvie held up a brindle. "Look at her ears!"

They were slightly mismatched, and the dog licked Sylvie's nose, wagging her tail enthusiastically. We all laughed.

"She's cute," Silas said, scratching the dog behind one of her lopsided ears.

Velma nodded. "That's Georgie. She's already had her first and second rounds of shots and is set to be spayed in nine months."

"For larger breeds, we wait until they're mature," I told Silas. "It minimizes the risk of certain health problems associated with early spaying."

"You could always foster," Vera said with a devious smile.

Sylvie hugged the puppy to her. Her smile was infectious. "We could do it together. I mean, who can ignore this face? And Walden needs a friend."

Her kitten had finally been given a proper name.

I wasn't sure if it was the puppy eyes Sylvie gave Silas or the actual dog's pleading look, but the big man caved, groaning as he ran a hand down his face. "Fine. Where do I sign up for this fostering thing?"

Vera and Velma exchanged a grin. Vera pulled a form out of her bag. "I've got the paperwork right here."

The rest of the day became chaotic with the puppy racing about underfoot until Silas bought her a playpen and set it up in the corner of the waiting room. Sylvie brought Walden in and introduced him to the puppy.

Mayhem took over.

But it was not the overwhelming kind like April Fools'

Day had brought. This was normal, and with all three of us doctors in the house, we ran like a well-oiled machine.

Near closing time, the Aldrich family stopped by. Redemption greeted me warmly, while Rena went right to Georgie and started playing with her. She loved on the kitten, too.

Roma handed me a floral arrangement. "We can't thank you enough for what you did."

The smell of sweet carnations and the sight of yellow roses reminded me of my mother's green thumb. Yellow roses had been a favorite of hers. "I'm so glad everything worked out okay. You *are* okay, right?"

Cormac nodded. "Killion has made sure we have everything we need to recover fully. Rena is still having nightmares, but they'll fade in time."

The girl climbed inside the playpen, laughing at Georgie's kisses. Redemption leaned over the plastic wall and sniffed the puppy, wagging his tail.

Silas, sitting in one of the waiting room chairs, smiled. "If there's anything I can do to help you out," he said to them, "please let me know."

Cormac nodded, and although I knew he didn't want Silas anywhere near his family, I appreciated him not saying so.

An hour after closing, I finished my paperwork and dictation. I made the rounds to ensure each room was prepped for the next day, and hummed to myself as I thought of the future of the clinic. My husband had emailed me the plans for a second clinic in a building he'd recently acquired. The rent would be low—as in free —but the renovation would require time and money.

Killion called it an 'investment' with a high ROI. I liked his perspective—it kept me from viewing the cost like a horror show.

When I returned to the office to shut off the lights and lock up, I found him, Ghost, and Corvus waiting for me.

"Miss Vera dropped off a casserole at the penthouse," he said with a quirk to his lips. "She asked Pennyworth what he was feeding you, since you looked like death warmed over. I fear my butler is scandalized."

I kissed him. "Never fear. I plan to eat everything he puts in front of me tonight."

Killion gave me a tantalizing look. "And after dinner?"

I removed my lab coat and grabbed my tote bag. "I could use a massage, a hot bath, and some uninterrupted time with my mate."

"I can guarantee all three."

With a glance at the photos of my parents on the wall, I blew each of them a kiss and took Killion's arm, feeling proud of my clinic and the work we were doing.

"Death called," Killion said as we climbed into the limo.

"I'm off duty tonight."

"Your new case can wait until tomorrow."

Since my boss had reached out to Killion first, I was curious. "Are you on this one, too?"

"I am, indeed. It's called a vacation."

I stiffened. "He's not using that as a euphemism for fired, right?"

Killion pulled me close. "No, my love. He wants you to take a few days to be normal. No grim work."

I drew back. "Death said that?"

"Yes." He tucked a piece of hair behind my ear. "He greatly appreciates what you've done, and with things in an uproar at SMG, much needs sorting out."

"But souls don't stop needing to be harvested."

"Diego is handling the immediate cases."

I laughed. "We'll see how that goes."

But for now, I had a few minutes, maybe even a few days of peace to look forward to.

Killion stroked my arm. "About that honeymoon we haven't taken yet..."

I leaned my head onto his shoulder. "Yes?"

"Perhaps we could escape for a few days to a secret lair of mine."

"Secret lair? Have you been holding out on me?"

That beautiful smile made an appearance. "I have."

I playfully smacked his chest. "Lord Reveux, you are a scoundrel."

LATER, I stepped out of the shower, wrapping a fluffy towel around my body and using another to squeeze the excess water from my hair. The steam followed me into the bedroom like a possessive ghost, dissipating only when I opened the door to find Killion waiting for me.

He stood by the open patio door, wearing a smoking jacket draped over his broad shoulders, and loose silk pants completing the look of casual elegance that only a three-hundred-year-old vampire could truly pull off. His dark eyes caught mine with a look that made my pulse quicken.

He disappeared into our walk-in closet, returning

with a simple sundress I'd bought on a whim last summer but had never worn. "This," he said, holding it out, "and nothing more."

My eyebrows shot up. "Does your secret lair require me to be half-naked?"

"We're not leaving the building." A smile played on his lips—the one that meant he was up to something. "And you won't be cold. I promise."

Curiosity piqued, I dropped my towel and slipped into the dress. The soft fabric clung to my still-damp skin. Killion watched with an appreciation that made me feel like the most beautiful woman in the world, despite my wet hair and lack of makeup.

"Close your eyes," he instructed, coming to stand behind me.

"This better not involve Pennyworth jumping out with a camera," I muttered, but closed my eyes anyway.

Killion's laugh was soft against my ear. His hands settled on my hips, warm and steady. "Keep them closed."

He guided me through our penthouse, and I heard the elevator doors sliding open. We stepped inside, and there was the subtle lurch as we ascended.

Ascended. Hmm. We were already on the top floor.

My bare feet against the cool floor, the warmth of Killion's body at my back, the scent of caramel and old books that followed him everywhere—my already fine-tuned senses heightened even more with my eyes closed. I was so grateful to have my magic back.

"Almost there," he murmured as the elevator doors opened, and a warm breeze caressed my face. We were outside? On the roof?

"Now," Killion said, guiding me out, "you can look."

I opened my eyes and gasped. The building's rooftop was a lush oasis, one I'd never seen before. Exotic plants in ornate pots created natural walls, their leaves rustling in the evening breeze. String lights wove through trellises overhead, casting a golden glow across the space. Plush outdoor furniture had been arranged in intimate groupings. In the center, a gleaming jacuzzi bubbled invitingly, steam rising into the night air.

"Do you like it?" There was a touch of vulnerability in his voice.

I turned to him, taking in his expectant expression. "Like it? This is *incredible*." I walked forward, trailing my fingers over the leaves of a plant with broad, tropical foliage. The entire ground beneath my feet was covered in soft moss. "When did you do all this?"

He followed me, watching my reactions. "Today. Pennyworth and I worked with a vampire landscaper who specializes in rooftop gardens. He included night-blooming plants."

"*Today*?" I moved to the edge of the roof, where a glass barrier provided safety without obstructing the view. Below us, Dante's Grove sprawled out in all its nighttime glory—a web of lights and shadows, life and hidden magic.

From here, you couldn't see the supernatural world that existed alongside the human one. It all looked normal. Mundane. And yet here we were, above it all. Killion, a master vampire, and me, his grim reaper tribrid wife, were creating paradise in the sky.

"It's the perfect contrast," I said, turning back to him.

"Down there is all our work, all the chaos and danger. And up here..."

"It's just us." He stepped closer, his hands finding my waist. "Our sanctuary."

The breeze lifted my damp hair, cooling my neck. "What about Ghost and Corvus? They'll love it up here."

"They've already given their approval. Ghost was particularly fond of that corner." He nodded toward a padded pet bed I hadn't noticed, positioned under a small canopy. "Corvus has claimed that perch." A tall, branching structure stood near another edge, perfect for my raven's watchful nature.

I laughed, imagining my Papillon mix prancing around the plants while my raven surveyed his new kingdom. "Of course they've already seen it."

"Master and Mistress?" Pennyworth's voice came from behind us. I turned to find him standing by a table I hadn't noticed, set with fine china, crystal glasses, and flickering candles. "Dinner is served."

"You think of everything," I whispered to Killion as he guided me to the table with a gentle hand at the small of my back.

"I've had centuries to learn the art of romance," he replied with a wink. "Though I must admit, none of my previous attempts have mattered as much as pleasing you."

The table was positioned to maximize our view of our private garden and the city beyond. Pennyworth served us with his usual efficient grace—a chilled soup to start, followed by herb-crusted lamb for Killion and a delicate sea bass for me. The wine was perfectly paired, and I knew without asking that it probably cost more than my monthly student loan payment.

"This is..." I shook my head, still amazed. "I don't even have words."

"That's a first." Killion's eyes crinkled at the corners. "Chloe Frost, rendered speechless."

"Chloe Frost-Reveux," I corrected, still not entirely used to my married name.

"Indeed." His smile deepened, satisfaction evident in every line of his face. "My wife, my mate."

We ate in comfortable silence, the city sounds a distant murmur beneath the gentle splash of the jacuzzi. Pennyworth cleared our main course and brought dessert, including white chocolate fudge cookies, a caramel mocha cake, and a tub of my favorite ice cream, which made me groan with pleasure.

Once we were alone again, Killion fed me from each dessert. "Tell me about the dragon fire," he said quietly.

The battle with the monster already seemed like ages ago. "It was..." I searched for words that could capture the essence of the experience. "It felt like drinking lightning. Every cell in my body was suddenly awake and singing." I took a cookie from him, breaking off a piece to feed to him. "I didn't know I could do that. Connect to your powers that way."

"They're part of you now." Killion's fingers traced the stem of his wine glass. "A non-dragon possessing them is unheard of."

"Well, we've never been conventional," I said with a chuckle. "Most women get a ring when they marry. I got the ability to breathe fire."

He chuckled, but his eyes remained thoughtful. "Were you frightened?"

"In the moment? No." I paused, considering. "I felt invincible. Like I could have torn down the world if I wanted to." I met his gaze directly. "It was intoxicating. A little terrifying in retrospect, but mostly amazing."

"And after?"

"I yearn for it," I admitted. "To try it again."

His hand covered mine on the table, warm and solid. "I don't want you taking unnecessary risks, and it *is* risky to use it."

I turned my hand to lace our fingers together. "I know. I won't."

He brought my hand to his lips, pressing a kiss to my knuckles. "We'll need to learn more about this aspect of our bond. How to feed it and control it."

"Add it to the list," I said lightly. "Right after 'learn to use scythe to cut pizza' and 'teach Ghost not to bark at invisible demons.'"

That earned me a genuine laugh, deep and rich. I loved that sound—it had been so rare when we first met, but I heard it more these days.

I turned my gaze back to the city, sipping my coffee. Only recently, I'd been a struggling veterinary student, grieving my parents, and struggling to get through each day. Now I was a qualified vet who moonlighted as a grim reaper, married to a master vampire with dragon blood, responsible for maintaining the supernatural balance in Danté's Grove.

Life had a weird way of working out.

"What are you thinking?" Killion asked.

"I'm thinking that if someone had told college-me where I'd end up, I would have laughed myself into a coma." I gestured toward the view. "Reaper. Mate. Guardian of this whole mess down there. It's a lot."

"Do you regret it?" The question was soft, undemanding.

I soaked in the face I'd come to love so profoundly—the sharp angles softened by affection, the power tempered by kindness. "Not for a second."

He stood, coming around the table and extending his hand. "Dessert can wait. The jacuzzi, however, cannot."

Shucking my dress while he poured us wine, I sank into the bubbling jacuzzi. The hot water soothed my muscles, and I leaned my head back against the edge, wine glass balanced precariously between my fingers.

Killion joined me, our shoulders touching beneath the churning water, his presence as comforting as the heat. The city sprawled below, oblivious to our private paradise, while stars winked overhead.

For once, I wasn't thinking about reaper duties or soul contracts or the menagerie of supernatural beings that seemed determined to make my life complicated. I was simply a woman enjoying a perfect evening with her husband.

Killion's fingers traced lazy patterns on my bare shoulder, sending pleasant shivers down my spine despite the hot water.

"You know what I miss sometimes?" I asked, taking another sip of the costly wine.

"Hmm?" His voice was a low rumble beside me.

"Ignorance. Before I knew about..."—I waved my free

hand vaguely at the night sky—"all of this. The supernatural. Death contracts. Dragons disguised as vampires."

Killion's voice was warm against my ear. "Would you go back? To not knowing?"

"No. But sometimes I miss when my biggest worry was passing my veterinary pharmacology exam."

"You were always meant for more than ordinary concerns, Chloe." His fingers slid up to the nape of my neck, gently massaging.

"Says the centuries-old vampire who was always born to rule." His eyes reflected in the soft lighting, and I stroked a finger across his forehead. "What did you think you were meant for when you were young?"

"Power," he answered without hesitation. "Wealth. Influence." His smile turned self-deprecating. "All the things a dragon lord's son is taught to value."

"And now?"

His expression softened. "Now I think perhaps I was simply meant to find you."

"There you are, being romantic again."

"I have my moments."

I let myself sink deeper into the water, my head resting on his shoulder. "I could get used to this," I said.

"That's the idea." His arm wrapped around me, pulling me closer. "We've earned some peace."

I raised my glass in salute. "To Undead ever after."

He clinked his goblet against mine. "Cute."

Footsteps approached—the measured, precise gait that could only belong to Pennyworth. "Mistress." His voice was a study in remorseful formality. "I apologize for the intrusion, but there is a call for you. I fear it may be urgent."

He stood rigidly at the edge of the jacuzzi area, my cell phone extended on a small silver tray, his gaze fixed determinedly at a point somewhere above our heads.

"Who is it?" Killion grumbled, not bothering to hide his annoyance.

"Andy." Pennyworth's expression seemed to convey his reluctance to be the bearer of bad news. Interesting that he assumed it was such.

I sat up, reaching for the phone. Water dripped from my arm onto the rooftop decking as I took it. "Thanks."

He nodded once and retreated a discreet distance, though I knew his supernatural hearing would pick up every word regardless.

"Andy, I'm on vacation," I said, trying not to sound as irritated as I felt. "This better be good."

Andy's easy-going tone was strained. "Sorry to bother you, but we've got a situation at Shepard's Rest. Again."

"What kind?" I asked, already knowing I wouldn't like the answer.

"Two shades showed up during the seven o'clock tour. They're making quite a scene—moving objects, dropping the temperature, freaking out the tourists. I've moved the tour group to the north section, but these two are following. They seem overly agitated, and I can't do anything for them."

The relaxing effects of the jacuzzi evaporated as quickly as the water droplets on my skin. "Have they hurt anyone?"

"Not yet, but they're getting stronger. I think they're feeding off the fear of the group."

I glanced at Killion, who was watching me with resignation in his eyes. He'd heard every word, of course. "Let it go for tonight," he said quietly. "Andy can handle it until morning."

I covered the phone with my hand. "You know I can't do that."

Andy seemed okay, even though his wolf was gone. I had the feeling Aurora was keeping him distracted. Still, I didn't want to leave him in a lurch.

"Tell him to call Diego," Killion countered.

"He's out of town, working on a case." It was up to me. Us. I uncovered the phone. "We'll be there in twenty minutes."

The relief in Andy's voice was palpable. "I owe you one."

"You owe me nothing. See you in a few." I hung up and looked regretfully at my wine glass. "Duty calls."

Killion's expression was unreadable for a moment before he sighed and stood up in a smooth motion, water cascading down his sculpted body. "Very well."

"You don't have to come," I offered, though I knew he would.

"And miss the opportunity to watch my wife wield her scythe?" He extended a hand to help me up. "I think not. It's downright sexy."

As I stood, I realized something that surprised me—I wasn't upset about needing to leave our perfect evening. There was a flutter of excitement in my stomach, a readiness. Somewhere along the line, this strange second career had become part of who I was, as natural as my veterinary work. Believing even for a few minutes that I'd lost my magic had made it seem all the more precious to me.

Pennyworth appeared with large, fluffy towels, still carefully averting his eyes. "Shall I prepare suitable attire for ghost hunting?" he asked.

"Please." I wrapped the towel around myself, suddenly shivering despite the warm night air. "And I'll need Ghost."

"Very good. The animal is currently napping in your bed. I shall wake her immediately."

I downed the remainder of my wine in one undignified gulp and headed for the elevator, Killion close behind. "Sorry about this," I said over my shoulder. "Rain check on our perfect evening?"

His hand caught mine, warm and reassuring. "I've never expected you to be anything other than exactly what you are."

The elevator doors closed behind us, and I leaned into him, damp skin against damp skin. "When did you become so understanding?"

"Around the time I realized I was in love with a woman who can't resist saving everyone and everything." His kiss was swift but tender. "Besides, I find your commitment to duty quite attractive."

Ten minutes later, I was dressed in what I jokingly called my "reaper chic" outfit—black jeans, sturdy boots, and a dark jacket that allowed for freedom of movement. My compact scythe was in its leather holder, waiting by the door.

Killion had changed into one of his impeccable dark suits—because vampires couldn't fight supernatural entities in casual wear.

Ghost trotted into the room, her small body vibrating with excitement. "Ready for work, girl?" I asked, and she yipped in response, dancing in circles around my feet.

Killion checked his watch. "If we leave now, we can be back within the hour."

"Optimistic." I grabbed the scythe and holder, feeling the familiar hum of power as it recognized my touch.

"Realistic," he countered. "Two shades shouldn't take long. You've handled worse in your sleep."

"True."

"The night is young," Killion said. "And watching you work has appeal."

"Flatterer."

"Honest vampire," he corrected, and pressed the button for the lobby.

26

Shepard's Rest welcomed us with the scent of damp earth and hanging moss. Moonlight spilled across ancient headstones and carved angels whose faces had been smoothed by decades of weather until they looked more alien than divine.

The massive wrought-iron gates creaked as we passed through them, as if the cemetery itself was announcing our arrival. Behind me, Ghost had already started her transformation, her small canine form elongating, fur brightening to an ethereal glow that cast shadows among the grave markers.

Killion moved silently at my side, his vampire senses scanning for threats beyond what humans could detect. I gripped my scythe, feeling the familiar weight settle into my palm like an extension of my arm. Just another night for the Reveuxs—date night interrupted by the inconveniently deceased.

Andy waited for us at the first fork in the path, his lanky frame leaning against a marble mausoleum.

Despite the situation, his expression remained characteristically laid-back, though I noticed the tension in his shoulders. "Thanks for coming," he said, pushing away from the concrete wall as we approached. "I convinced the leader of the tour group to head over to the founders' section with some story about a special midnight viewing of the mayor's great-grandfather's grave." He shrugged. "People eat that historical stuff up."

"And the shades?" Killion asked.

Andy pointed toward a cluster of older graves surrounded by a wrought-iron fence. "Over there. They started by following us, making cold spots. Now they're knocking over flowers, scratching at headstones. One of the tourists got pushed—nothing serious, but it freaked everyone out."

My grave sight kicked in. "I see them." I adjusted my grip on the scythe. "Two of them, right?"

"Yeah," Andy confirmed. "I can see them. Some weird effect from one of Aurora's teas, I think. Usually I can smell them, but after what happened..." He trailed off, and there it was—the sense of loss over his wolf. He recovered quickly, though. "Both male, from what I can tell. They appear to be recent deaths."

"Keep the tourists occupied," I instructed. "We'll handle this."

Andy hesitated, glancing at Ghost. "Need any backup?"

"We've got it," I assured him.

He backed away, casting one last look at the area where the shades lingered. "I'll keep the living on the north side for another thirty minutes. That enough time?"

Killion answered before I could. "More than sufficient."

As Andy jogged away, I turned to Killion. "Perimeter?"

He nodded. While I handled the shades, he would ensure no other supernatural entities decided to join the party—and that no curious humans wandered into the strike zone.

I approached the fenced area with Ghost at my heels. The first shade materialized fully as I approached—a young man in an Army uniform, his face a mask of confusion and anger. Blood covered a neck wound and ran down to his jacket.

The second shade was a middle-aged man in jeans and a flannel shirt, a gaping wound in his chest suggesting a violent end.

"Hello, gentlemen," I called out, stepping around a marker. "You're causing quite a disturbance tonight. It's time for you to move on."

The soldier turned toward me, his eyes widening as he registered my scythe and Ghost's supernatural form. "Reee...per," he hissed, the word distorted.

"That's right," I confirmed. "And you're overdue for a crossing."

The other shade backed away, but the soldier advanced, his form flickering. Objects around him began to shake—fallen leaves swirled upward, small stones rattled against headstones.

"Won't go," he snarled. "Not done. Not ready."

"Your soul contract wasn't up, and I'm sorry you died

prematurely, but this is the only way. You have to move to the afterlife. Trust me, it's nice there. You'll like it."

My senses picked up on the tethers that kept these shades bound to the mortal plane. Every lingering soul had them, be they emotional connections, unfinished business, or sometimes just plain stubbornness.

The soldier's ties were strong, thick cords of regret and vengeance. The older man's were more tenuous, suggesting he might be easier to persuade.

I decided to start with him. "You," I pointed my scythe at him. "What's keeping you here?"

He flickered nervously, eyes darting between me and the exit. "My wife," he mumbled. "I need to tell her that it wasn't her fault."

Ah. A classic. "Accident?" I asked.

He shrugged. "Car. Black ice. She was driving."

"And she blames herself." I took a step closer. Ghost circled behind him, creating a barrier to prevent his escape. "What's your name?"

"Nate," he muttered. "Nate Dennings."

"Well, Nate, I have good news and bad news." I lowered my scythe slightly, adopting a less threatening stance. "The bad news is, you're definitely dead, and it's time to move on. The good news is, I can help you leave a message."

The soldier shade shrieked, apparently displeased with my attention to Nate rather than him. A nearby vase of flowers exploded, sending petals and water flying in all directions.

"Wait your turn," I ordered, and a vibration pulsed through the cemetery.

To my surprise, he subsided.

Good.

Nate's form steadied, hope making him more substantial. "You can tell her?"

The ability to negotiate these small mercies was a perk of my job. Death might be inevitable, but sometimes I could ease the transition. "Give me her name and contact info, and I'll be sure to pass on your message."

"Elaine Dennings. 42 Maple Street." His voice grew stronger as he committed to the decision. "Tell her it was no one's fault. It wasn't her driving. She shouldn't blame herself. And...tell her I love her."

I nodded, memorizing the details. "She'll know. Now, are you ready?"

He took what would have been a deep breath if he still needed to breathe. "Ready."

I held out the scythe, and I saw his eyes soften. In this moment, most people saw something comforting, usually food, and had the natural inclination to reach for it. Whatever he saw did the trick. He touched it, and the blade did its thing, dividing the lingering spiritual energy from its earthly attachments. Ghost gently took his spirit, smiling now, across the veil.

One down, one to go.

I turned to the soldier, who had watched the proceedings with growing agitation. "Your turn."

"No!" His shout echoed through the cemetery. "I'm not finished! I want to live!"

This was going to be the hard way, then. "I know you do. I know this is the hardest thing you've ever done. Is there anyone on the other side who's waiting for you? A grandparent? A pet who's passed?"

His eyes blazed with spectral fire. "I'm not going."

"Your anger only hurts you."

"Not only me." His mouth twisted into a grotesque smile. "I can hurt the living. Make them feel what I feel."

And there it was—the reason shades became dangerous. When a spirit lingered, feeding on negative emotions, it could develop the ability to cause real harm. This one was further along that path than I'd initially thought.

"Not on my watch." I twirled the scythe, feeling its power respond to my intent. "I don't need your cooperation," I informed him, advancing with the scythe raised. "Though it would be easier on both of us."

The shade lashed out, a burst of spectral energy that would have knocked a normal person off their feet. The energy simply washed over me, cold but ultimately harmless.

Killion appeared beside me, moving so quickly he seemed to materialize from the shadows. "Assistance?" he offered mildly, though I could see the tension in his stance.

"Just keep the perimeter secure," I told him. "This one's stubborn, but not beyond my skills."

The shade threw another burst of energy, this time directed at a nearby headstone. The stone cracked with a sound like a gunshot.

"Enough," I said, no longer patient. Ghost reappeared. I rushed the soldier, bringing the scythe across his body in a decisive arc.

He tried to dodge, but Killion was there, sending his magic out in a wall that the shade couldn't penetrate. He had nowhere to go.

The blade passed through him, and he screamed—a sound that echoed through the grounds and probably gave Andy's tour group another genuine paranormal experience to talk about.

Unlike Nate's peaceful dissolution, this shade fought the process. Ghost had to work harder, grabbing his spirit by the scruff and shaking it before she and the shade disappeared.

As we waited for her second return, Andy approached cautiously from the direction of the tour group. "All clear?"

"All clear," I confirmed, straightening up. "Your tourists might have heard the second one's exit, though. Could make for good publicity."

He grinned. "Already spinning it as 'authentic paranormal activity.' The tour guide is thrilled. Says it's their most interactive experience to date."

"Glad to be of service to the local tourism economy," I said dryly.

As Andy jogged back to his group, Killion turned me to face him, his eyes scanning for any sign of injury. Finding none, he pulled me into his arms and kissed me. There, under the moonlight and surrounded by centuries of the dead, he took my breath away.

When we finally parted, I blinked up at him. "What was that for?"

"For being mine," he replied. "For being capable and compassionate, even with those who don't deserve it."

"Sweet talking me in a graveyard?"

His eyes darkened with lust and desire. "Ready to finish our honeymoon?"

The question hung between us, charged with promise. Around us, the cemetery had settled back into its peaceful slumber, the disruption of the shades now just another story in its long history.

"Yes," I said, slipping my hand into his. My scythe, its work done, settled contentedly in its leather holder. Ghost, back and fully returned to her small dog form, yipped happily at our feet.

Killion's thumb traced circles on the back of my hand, a small gesture that somehow contained all the intimacy of our interrupted evening. "Think the jacuzzi water's still hot?" I asked as we reached his limo. Moss jumped out and opened the door for us.

"If not, we'll heat it again." He ushered me in with old-world courtesy. "We have all night."

Ghost jumped in, curling up as if she hadn't just escorted two souls to the afterlife. Killion and I slid in beside her, getting a head start on our raincheck as we pulled away from Shepard's Rest, our rooftop paradise beckoning.

Some might find it strange, this life we'd built together, balancing duty and desire, death and life. But as Killion's soul reached for mine, I couldn't imagine wanting anything else.

FREE URBAN FANTASY! GET REVENGE IS SWEET, KALI SWEET URBAN FANTASY FREE

*S*tep into the thrilling world of the *Kali Sweet* series—a snarky, fast-paced urban fantasy adventure packed with vampires, shifters, demons, angels, and a fierce heroine you won't forget!

If you're a fan of paranormal books featuring strong female leads with razor-sharp wit, sizzling romance, and jaw-dropping twists, this series is for you.

Dive into a world where the supernatural collides with high-stakes drama. Kali Sweet isn't your typical heroine—she's a no-nonsense, supernatural-busting force to be reckoned with. Whether she's outsmarting vampires, taking down rogue shifters, or facing off against celestial beings, Kali's brand of snark and courage will have you hooked from page one.

Fans of urban fantasy series like *The Dresden Files*, *Mercy Thompson*, or *Kate Daniels* will love the Kali Sweet series. Watch now to experience the magic, humor, and danger that define this unforgettable paranormal universe.

📚 Don't miss the chance to start your next favorite urban fantasy series. Grab your FREE copy of Revenge Is Sweet today!

https://marketplace.curios.com/collections/0xb9b5e7f24995c5d99855d07d5af82001b9330a2a

VISIT MY STORE

Did you know you can buy directly from me? When you do, the retailer doesn't take a cut and I can pass on the savings to YOU!

https://mistyevansbooks.com/shop

Benefits:

You can find ALL my books in one place

SAVE money

EARLY access to new releases

Special Collections, Boxed eSets, and Limited Editions

Support a small business (and support a dream!)

Why Buy Direct?

When you purchase a book by your favorite author, electronic or print, on retailer platforms, the company keeps 30-70% of the sale, leaving the author with little to no profit (after the company deducts delivery fees, taxes, and other fees).

Buying directly from the author means that more goes to them so they can keep turning out stories for you. Every published story, every book, requires cover art, editing, and hours and hours of the author's time simply to create it. Not to mention overhead costs, such as websites, newsletters, writing software, graphics programs, advertising, taxes, etc.

In addition, one of the big-name retailers requires exclusivity, and all of them have terms of service and rules and regulations that make it challenging and time-consuming for an indie author to navigate the publishing world.

Most of us would MUCH rather spend our time creating more stories for YOU, rather than trying to jump through the hoops at the retailers. Buying direct from your favorite authors (where available) helps ensure that an author you love is not subject to unexplained account closures, withholding of royalties, censorship, and other issues that can affect their livelihood.

I've experienced ALL of these. By buying direct, you help put control of my work back in my hands - and I can continue to write more.

Either way, thank you for supporting me! I under-stand buying direct doesn't work for everyone and even if you use the retailers to buy my books, I appreciate you!

Happy reading,

Misty

https://mistyevansbooks.com/shop

PNR & UF BY MISTY/NYX HALLIWELL

The Accidental Reaper Series, available in ebook, print, and audio

Grim & Bare It, Book 1

Reaper's Keepers, Book 2

In too Reap, Book 3

Killin' It (short story for newsletter subscribers only)

The Vampire's Kiss (an exclusive short story available in Misty's Store. *Intended for mature audiences 17+)*

Grave Girl

Grave Magic

Grim Vows

Undead Ever After

Listen to the series on the Eleven Reader Publishing App!

The Kali Sweet Series, available in ebook and print! Coming soon to audio.

Revenge Is Sweet, Kali Sweet Series, Book 1

Sweet Chaos, Kali Sweet Series, Book 2

Sweet Soldier, Kali Sweet Series, Book 3

Sweet Curse, Kali Sweet Series, Book 4

Sweet Malice, Kali Sweet Series, Book 5

Sweet Betrayal, Kali Sweet Series, Book 6 (coming winter of 2025)

Witches Anonymous Step 1

Jingle Hells, WA Step 2

Wicked Souls, WA Step 3

Dark Moon Lilith, Witches Anonymous Step 4

Dancing With the Devil, Witches Anonymous Step 5

Devil's Due, Witches Anonymous Step 6

Dirty Deeds, Witches Anonymous Step 7

Wicked Wedding, Witches Anonymous Step 8

Soul Survivor, Moon Water Series, Book 1

Soul Protector, Moon Water Series, Book 2

COZY MYSTERIES (WRITING AS NYX HALLIWELL)

Sister Witches Of Raven Falls Mystery Series

Of Potions and Portents

Of Curses and Charms

Of Stars and Spells

Of Spirits and Superstition

Confessions of a Closet Medium Series

Sister Witches of Story Cove Series

Cinder

Belle

Snow

Ruby

Zelle

Sister Witches of Story Cove Complete Set

***

Witchy Candy Shop Mysteries

Tricks and Treats

Candy and Creeps

Gum and Ghouls

THRILLING ROMANTIC SUSPENSE & MYSTERIES

Don't want to miss a single release? Sign up for my newsletter at www.mistyevansbooks.com

Black Swan Division Romantic Thriller Series

Redeeming Meg

Tempting Tessa

Avenging Jessie

SEALs of Shadow Force Series

Fatal Truth

Fatal Honor

Fatal Courage

Fatal Love

Fatal Vision

Fatal Thrill

Risk

SEALS of Shadow Force Series: Spy Division

Man Hunt

Man Killer

Man Down

Operation Proof of Life

Operation Lost Princess

Operation Ambush

Operation Contraband

Operation Sleeping With the Enemy

Operation Heist

The Justice Team Series (with Adrienne Giordano)

Stealing Justice

Cheating Justice

Holiday Justice

Exposing Justice

Undercover Justice

Protecting Justice

Missing Justice

Defending Justice

SCHOCK SISTERS MYSTERY SERIES w/Adrienne Giordano

1st Shock

2nd Strike

3rd Tango

The Secret Ingredient Culinary Mystery Series

The Secret Ingredient, A Culinary Romantic Mystery with Bonus Recipes

The Secret Life of Cranberry Sauce, A Secret Ingredient Holiday Novella

I HAVE A SECRET TO SHARE
WITH YOU

A little dream of mine has been growing quietly for a while now, and I'm finally ready to share it with you.

I've been working on a secret project that's especially dear to me—something tender, nostalgic, and full of heart. It's called **Letters From Gram**.

Growing up, I experienced a profound absence. My paternal grandmother, Gertrude Anne, passed away when I was only two years old. I'm told she was short like me and had a passion for poetry—sometimes I wonder if my love of writing is a thread connecting us across time.

My maternal grandmother, Eunice, lived far away, and I only saw her once or twice a year before she passed away before my 18th birthday.

I never truly got to know either of them.

Throughout my life, I've felt the absence of that special grandmother relationship—someone I could call when I needed encouragement, someone who would offer wisdom about life's complexities, careers, relationships, and love.

To fill this void, I began writing letters to myself from an imaginary grandmother, creating the nurturing voice I longed to hear.

These personal letters became a source of comfort and guidance during challenging times, and I realized I wasn't alone in this longing. Many of us yearn for a loving family connection—a gentle voice of experience sharing both practical advice and emotional support. Others of us miss those connections after our loved ones have passed on.

That's why I created Letters From Gram. Each letter is crafted with the same care and attention I put into the ones I write for myself, offering a grandmother's wisdom and warmth that so many of us seek, or miss because our own grandmothers have passed on.

My hope is that these letters bring you comfort, joy, and the feeling of connection that comes from knowing someone cares about your journey.

When you receive a Letter From Gram, you're

receiving a piece of the grandmother relationship I've always imagined—and perhaps one you've longed for (or missed), too.

Through Letters From Gram, subscribers receive monthly physical letters, charming notes, and even tiny surprise gifts from Gram and her two cats, Marmalade and Swiftie.

It's a slow moment in a fast world, a cozy hug in an envelope.

• Make going to the mailbox fun again. You'll receive an uplifting letter each month for an entire year.

• Each letter is meticulously written, crafted, and thoughtfully designed by me.

• Each envelope includes a gift from Gram - her favorite recipes, pressed flowers from her garden, charms, tea bags, and more that turn a simple letter into an **enhanced experience.**

• Letters From Gram is a bright spot amongst bad news, bills, and junk mail. Now, you can enjoy a hug, love, and small tokens from a grandmotherly figure.

A dash of old-fashioned wisdom. A sprinkle of kindness. A mailbox full of heart.

Gram's mission, and mine, is to remind you that you're loved, you matter, and someone out there is rooting for you—always. Twelve letters a year will make going to the mailbox fun again and remind you of how important you are in this world.

Because sometimes, what you need most is a hug.

I'd be honored if you'd take a look and let me know what you think. https://lettersfromgram.com

I'm dedicating Letters From Gram to Gertrude Anne and Eunice.

Share this with anyone you think could use a boost. Let's start a movement to bring love and kindness back into our world.

Misty

MEET MISTY

USA TODAY Bestselling Author Misty Evans is celebrating her 100th published novel in 2025. She loves writing urban fantasy, paranormal romance, and mystery/suspense. Under her pen name, Nyx Halliwell, she also writes supernatural cozy mysteries.

When not reading or writing (which is most of the time), she enjoys music, movies, and hanging out with her husband, twin sons, and three spoiled rescue dogs. She's a crafter at heart and has far too many projects to finish.

Visit www.mistyevansbooks.com to check out her online store and sign up for her newsletter.

LETTER FROM MISTY

Thank you for reading this story! It is an honor and a privilege to write books for you. I'm an indie author and every fan is important to me. I pour my heart into each story and do my best to bring you an escape from the real world.

Readers are the key to my success - not a traditional publishing deal (had four), an agent (had two), or a publicity team (yep, you guessed it, had several of those as well.)

Those of you who read my books, love my characters and worlds, and then tell others about them are the best of friends. I adore you and will keep writing if you keep reading!

If you'd like to learn about my other books, sales, and special promotions, please sign up for my newsletter at **www.mistyevansbooks.com**.

You'll get coupons to download starter packs for FREE, whether you love my suspense or my paranormal.

Support me directly (no retailer taking their cut), grab special edition box sets, and get new releases before they are out at retailers by visiting my store **https://mistyevans books.com/shop.**

I have sales and offer NEW RELEASES early! Check it out.

Last but not least, if you enjoy clean, cozy mysteries, visit my pen name **www.nyxhalliwell.com** to see those books.

Thank you, and happy reading!

Misty